'I'll be the brightest star...'

A novel by

Philip Howells

Dedicated to the memory of my father, David Baden Howells,
who illuminated my life so brightly but for so little time.

First edition published December 2019

Chapter 1: Siôn, Nest and Caroline

The year was 1846. Autumn had arrived in South Wales early and the trees in Newchurch in Carmarthenshire, had already turned golden brown but this day it was dull, raining and wintery. All his life Siôn Lewis had lived within 15 miles of the farm he now rented, just as his father and grandfather had before him. His work too had changed little in all that time. A few more machines perhaps and better tools and implements but otherwise the Wheel of Fortune had turned very slowly in this part of rural Wales. The gentle, rolling hills carved over the centuries by narrow streams had been almost unchanged despite the industrial upheaval just 50 miles to the east. There the valleys were now black with waste from the coal mines, tipped layer upon layer so that the green hills were now grim, black mountains.

Nest, his wife was waiting for Siôn in the kitchen after he removed his muddy boots in the scullery.

'Before you get washed and changed,' said his wife diffidently, 'Caroline needs to talk to you.'

Siôn slipped off the heavy oilskin coat and hat the weather had demanded that day and hung it in the porch to drip. He pulled off his woollen hat and dropped it on the fire dog in the hearth beside his chair.

'Something important?' Siôn enquired, quite used to dealing with the passing caprices of his 21 year-old daughter, the oldest of their children.

'I'll let her explain herself.'

'Very well. Ask her to come down,' he said loosening the buttons of his thick work shirt and warming his hands by the fireside. Nest untied her apron, dusted down her skirts, left the room and climbed the stairs to the family's sleeping rooms on the first floor above the byre.

'Your father's home,' she said to her daughter who lay on her bed, sobbing her heart out. 'Soonest told, soonest mended.'

'Will you come with me Mam?' asked Caroline, straightening her full skirt of coarse, fawn cotton and tucking her blouse in at the waist.

'No, you need to talk to him yourself. Go on.'

Her daughter carefully descended the narrow stairs and closed the kitchen door behind her. Nest sat on the bed and listened carefully. She heard only muffled voices until, after a pause, her husband raised his voice to a shout. This was so unusual for him, Nest feared for the worst.

'You're what?' Caroline's father exploded. The colour drained from his face as the seriousness of his daughter's news sank in. Normally calm, even stoic, his voice rose and stuttered briefly in shock. He sat forward in his chair and grasped the table to steady himself as he stood up staring angrily and almost disbelievingly at his daughter.

'I'm pregnant Dada. I... I'm going to have a baby,' she stammered as she stared ashamedly at the stone floor of their cottage kitchen, unable to look at her father as she gripped the back of the kitchen chair beside her so tightly her knuckles were white.

'Yes, I know what being pregnant means my girl, it's just that I never expected to hear you say it 'less you were married. Who's the father?'

Caroline paused. Siôn gasped for breath, looked up at the ceiling, then directly at his daughter. Again he asked, 'Who is the father, Caroline?'

Without raising her eyes, her fingers wrapping her handkerchief tightly around her hands, she mumbled, 'I don't know Dada,' before bursting into tears again.

Her father stepped back visibly shocked and stumbled awkwardly against the kitchen table. For several minutes Caroline sobbed as quietly as she could, her hands still clasped tightly in front of her while her father stared into space above him as he absorbed the news his daughter had just given him.

Eventually Siôn spoke. 'I don't understand. I read in the newspaper about tarts and actresses and even some royalty leading such licentious lives they don't know who's fathered their children but I never expected a daughter of mine to be in that position.' Siôn's breathing was ragged and laboured. Suddenly, realising he might have misunderstood his daughter's situation and jumped to the wrong conclusion, he spoke more understandingly, 'or are you saying Caroline, you were raped? Did men gang up and abuse you?'
Caroline shook her head and wept even louder.

'Then I just don't know what to think,' continued her father shaking his head in disbelief. 'You willingly let men take advantage of you and you don't know the name of any of them? What sort of girl are you?'

Caroline continued to cry as her father went on, his words now tumbling from his mouth. 'Does your mother know? Or have you being keeping this from both of us?'
Caroline nodded briefly. 'Mam knows. She said to tell you'.

'And rightly so, but so far you've told me almost nothing.'
Caroline sobbed even more deeply. Her father continued, 'Well clearly I'm not going to get any sense out of you at the moment. Best you go to your mother and when you can stop crying come back and talk to me again. Go on.'

Caroline turned abruptly and, with some relief, hurried from the kitchen. Her father was torn between raging anger at the men who'd abused his daughter and, almost at the same time, his heart trembled with sadness for the plight in which his own first-born had been placed. Deciding that hard work might be one way to help him deal with a situation he never thought he'd have to face, he pulled his boots back on, took his oilskin coat and hat from the hook and walked out across the yard into the rain. In the barn he continued to fork the last of the previous autumn's hay into one of the empty stalls, his anger and disappointment driving the fury with which he cleared the dried grass. Even when a nest of rats broke out from the corner in which they'd been hiding and dodged the thrust of his pitchfork, he kicked wildly at the vermin that scurried to safety out of the barn doorway.

It was after 8pm before Siôn returned to the farmhouse, got washed and changed, ready to eat his evening meal in the kitchen. By then his wife had already fed Caroline and her three younger, teenage brothers. All four children were employed on the farm, the boys working in the fields like their father, Caroline helping her mother with domestic chores around the farmhouse and assisting her father in the dairy. That evening, to avoid speaking to Caroline, he'd asked Rhys, his eldest boy, to help him with the milking and, though his son realised this request foretold a serious family argument, he complied without question.

After his meal Siôn sat silently as his wife cleared the table. Nest returned with their old brown pottery teapot and placed it between them on the table. Siôn broke his silence.

'You know everything, I assume?' he asked.

'I know what she's told me which is probably not much more than she's told you.'

'All she's said to me is that she's going to have a baby,' said Siôn, 'and either doesn't know or wouldn't tell me who the father is.'

'She doesn't know,' said Nest flatly, stirring the teapot before replacing the cracked lid.

'What sort of a daughter have we brought up that gets pregnant yet doesn't know who's the father?'

'It's not as simple as that Siôn,' replied Nest calmly.

'Then perhaps she'll tell me how complicated it is then. Where is she? Let her come to me now and explain.'

'Will you listen or just shout at her?'

'Don't you think I have a right to shout?' he said abruptly then paused, his breathing irregular again. 'What sort of man do you think I am Nest? It happens I care who lies down with my daughter and gets her pregnant so, sorry if you think I shouldn't be angry. But I'll

4

hear her out. Bring her down.'

Nest finished pouring their tea then left the kitchen and climbed the crude stairs to the bedrooms.

'Your dada wants to talk to you again,' she said.

Caroline preceded her mother downstairs into the kitchen, still shaking and red-eyed. Her father motioned for her to stand beside her mother on the opposite side of the table. Speaking in his more usual, placid, voice he turned to his daughter.

'Your mother said the matter of your baby's father is complicated. I need to understand.' Caroline looked toward her mother who inclined her head in Siôn's direction indicating Caroline should speak to her father.

'Well Dada, I met this man back in May at Carmarthen Horse Fair...'

'*Duw*, not an Irish tinker, surely?' Siôn interrupted abruptly.

'Hear her out Siôn,' said Nest trying to calm the moment.

'OK,' then to his daughter, 'go on.'

'Yes, Dada he's Irish but not a tinker, his father's a horse dealer.' Siôn exhaled and shook his head.

Caroline continued, her voice becoming more controlled as she spoke. 'Michael, that's his name, is a lovely man, honestly Dada, and he took me out every day of the fair.'

'I thought you said you were staying with your cousin, Ffion, all that time?'

'I was living at Ffion's but I met Michael the second day I was at the fair.'

Siôn shook his head in disbelief and muttered, 'More lies.'

Caroline slumped down on the kitchen chair beside her mother, the pleats of her blouse damp with her tears.

'I'm sorry Dada, but I was in love with him, honestly.'

'So how come you don't know who's the father of your baby, then?' said Siôn, leaning forward towards his daughter to emphasise his question.

'It happened because of Michael's older brother, Francis. He caught us in the family's tent where they'd been living down by the river during the fair. He told Michael their father wanted to talk to him at the buying ring and, when Michael had gone, pushed me back in the tent. Told me that if I was OK for Michael, I was just as good for him. He forced me Dada. Honestly I tried to stop him but he was too strong and horrible.'

'Does the brother know this?'

'Yes I told him next time I saw him. There was a terrible fight and Francis got knifed.'

'An' this is the type of man you'd have for your baby's father, an Irish knife-fighter?'

'He wasn't that at all,' she said her voice pleading with her father for his understanding. 'It was Francis had the knife. Michael only used it after his brother dropped it.'

'An' where are they now?'

'They're back in Kerry. Their father took them home with him the next day.'

'Nice family too, both the Irish rapists taken out of the country leaving you with their bastard child.'

Caroline broke down and started crying again at her father's use of the word. Nest had sat silent and still throughout this exchange. When her daughter turned to her for comfort she wrapped her beige woollen shawl around Caroline's shoulders and held her hand on the table but declined to give her any more physical comfort. For some minutes the three of them sat silent save for Caroline's crying, then Siôn got up from the table.

'Well I'm going to bed. Your mother and I will talk more on this and let you know what we decide. Till then, 'less you want to bring any more shame on me and your mam than you already have, you'll not say anything of it to anyone–and that includes your brothers. Your mam and me will tell you when we've decided what to do.'

'Of course Dada. I am so sorry,' said Caroline as her father rose from the table and walked from the room leaving his wife comforting her daughter crying against her shoulder yet again.

The following day Siôn spoke very little and didn't mention the subject to his wife or his daughter. In fact for the next four days he said little about anything to any of his family. All they got were long silences though Nest knew their daughter was never far from his mind. Finally, as the farmer strolled home from Morning Worship at chapel the following Sunday with his wife on his arm, he spoke.

'This jacket's getting a bit tight, Ness,' he said using his wife's favourite nickname. 'I must be getting a bit fat.' He pulled at the waist of the jacket of his black Sunday-best suit.

'Or a bit older?' smiled Nest, squeezing his arm as they walked. In truth she'd been aware as most women are that she and her husband were beginning to show their age, not that they were old. As he approached 50 his height–he was over 6ft–disguised the slight increase in his waist. His hair was still thick and dark, his gait upright and straight and he could manage a long day's work at harvest without over-tiring himself. The years had been less kind to Nest. Standing a full 9 inches shorter than her husband and after bearing four children, her slightly plump figure was more noticeable. Not that Siôn was bothered. Her hair was still as wavy and silky as when they'd married even though a few grey hairs had become entwined with her dark Celtic locks. They'd always been compatible in bed and enjoyed a satisfying harmony that had seen them through the usual share of trials couples had to face. But the latest was one they'd not prepared for.

'It's a mess all right, isn't it Ness?'

'It is that Siôn *bach*, there's no denying it'.

'Do we have any options, really?' he asked.

'Not really,' replied his wife, 'not if you're the kind of man I thought I'd married.'

'What you mean by that?'

'Well, to be brutal, it means we've got two choices,' said Nest arranging her shawl around her shoulders and folding her arms in front of her.

'Yes?'

'We either send her away to find somewhere else to live,

have her baby and fend for herself or she has the baby here and we take care of it.'

'There's certainly a brutal choice,' replied her husband. 'Are you prepared to send her away and never see her again?'

Nest paused, thinking but not speaking before she continued.

'Look I know you're angry, we both are. We brought our daughter up to be better than this and she's let us, and herself, down badly. But she's still our daughter and under your anger, our anger, we both still love her.'

'You're right, of course, but where does that take us?' They stopped walking and Siôn cleared dead leaves and bark chips from a fallen tree trunk so that Nest wouldn't dirty her best skirt as they sat side-by-side.

After a few minutes silence Nest spoke again, more quietly and gently, 'She's our only daughter, Siôn. She's been very foolish and made a mistake she'll have to live with the rest of her life but she's still ours.'

'So we just live with the shame?' continued Siôn picking idly at the roughness around the ends of his fingers.

'The shame depends on who knows, what they know and, more importantly, what they think and whether we care what they think.' Siôn was silent. 'Let's walk on *bach*,' said Nest. When they reached the farm all their children were out of the house, so they continued their conversation in the kitchen. 'And one thing you and I should remember Siôn before we start getting self-righteous about this,' said Nest, 'we need to remember how it was for us before we were married.' She leant forward to hold Siôn's hand across the table. 'What would we have done if I'd got pregnant then?'

'Yes but we were intending to get married anyway, Ness.'

'Of course we were. We were in love but Caroline thought she was in love too. We'd have had to have moved if you'd made me pregnant wouldn't we?' asked Nest knowingly.

'Perhaps, but not necessarily,' countered Siôn defensively but grudgingly too.

'You want a cup of tea *bach*?' asked Nest.

'OK, go on.'

'Of course,' continued Nest, 'Caroline'd have to stay out of sight and not go into the village but we could say she was poorly. Then, from the time she showed until she had the baby I'd have to find a place for her to stay in Carmarthen somewhere.'

'What then?'

'Then we'd bring the baby up as one of our family. We'd tell people it was the baby of a cousin who died giving birth and that we've adopted her baby.'

'What you and me?'

'Certainly, why not?' Nest poured the tea into their cups and added milk and sugar. 'We wouldn't be the first family in that situation and I doubt we'll be the last.'

'Well if you think we could get away with it...' said Siôn cautiously as he stirred his tea.

'As I say we wouldn't be the first and if people want to think the worst about us well, they're probably going to do that anyway.'

'Shall I talk to Caroline?' asked Siôn.

'Leave her to me. What you need to do is take care of the boys. They're much more likely to gossip than you or me or Caroline.'

'But there's no reason they should know until later,' said Siôn, 'I'll talk to them then. For now we need to make sure Caroline agrees with your plan, *our* plan,' said Siôn emphasising the point with his forefinger on the table.

'Exactly, *our* plan,' said Nest with determination and some finality.

Early the following week, while Siôn and the boys were away driving a small herd of sheep to market in Carmarthen, Nest told Caroline what she and Siôn had decided.

'Oh *diolch* Mam,' said Caroline, embracing her mother.

'Hold on, my girl. That doesn't mean we're happy about the situation nor that it's going to be easy.'

'No, but it's not what I was afraid of.'

'What do you mean?'

'I thought you'd force me to give the baby away, or even worse to have gone to one of those awful witches back of Burry Port with their potions and knitting needles.'

'You obviously have a pretty poor opinion of me and your father if you think we'd do that. Despite your foolishness maybe you'll begin to understand the sort of people we really are–and respect us for it.'

'Oh Mam, I do, really I do.'

'Well it's not going to be easy. People come and go every day and in a village idle tongues have little to do but wag. You'll be lucky if you can keep it a secret once you start to show.'

'I thought about that but at least by then winter'll be coming on so everyone'll be wearing more clothes.'

'That's true but it's not just your belly that gets fat when you're with a child, it'll show in your face too–an' there's nothing like an evil tongue to start rumours. No my girl, next year isn't going to be easy for you.'

'I'll do me best Mam, I really will.'

A couple of months later when Siôn and his sons were clearing a stream in the bottom field, the four had stopped for a break at midday and he raised the question of their sister's pregnancy. Rhys, leant against the fence eating a lump of cheese and a slice of dark bread. At 19 he was only a couple of years younger than Caroline and obviously understood the seriousness of the situation. It was Oswain and Daniel's smirks Siôn had to deal with.

'If you two think this is funny I assure you you'll be laughing the other side of your faces when people start pointing at you in the street and telling dirty jokes about your sister,' said Siôn to them firmly, pointing to each in turn as they sat on a log, to underline his point. 'What I want from you now is a bit of maturity and a bit of respect for your mother and me. Caroline's been foolish and made a mistake but your mother and I are standing by her. She's family and deserves our support. If we aren't going to be there for her who is?

10

She's made one mistake, just one. If either of you thinks you can get through the rest of your lives and make just one mistake then go ahead and laugh. Laugh all you want but I tell you what boys, that laugh is one you'll regret as long as you live. As sure as God made little apples, that's a fact. Trust me.'

'Sorry Dada,' said Daniel who'd be 15 later that year and was the youngest and more embarrassed than amused. Rhys continued to stare at the ground in front of him, while Oswain only a year younger than Rhys but with much the same build and constantly competing with his older brother, idly pushed the tines of his fork in and out of the grassy bank on which he was sitting. His emotionless countenance revealing to anyone who looked how his secret indifference towards his sister affected his view of her situation. Siôn noticed as any father would and thought to himself "that's where the trouble will be, with Oswain," but he said nothing.

'So we're agreed,' continued Siôn. 'You've all known since you were kids how babies are made. You've seen lots of animals born here on the farm, and a few that didn't make it. You know what's involved and I'm counting on you all being grown up about Caroline and her *baban* when it comes.'

In fact Caroline was almost 6 months gone before anyone spoke directly to the family and then to no one's surprise, especially Nest's, it was Alys Pritchard, the self-righteous, busybody wife of the Methodist pastor when they met in the village.

'Not seen your Caroline recently, Mrs Lewis. Everything is okay with her?'

'She's fine thank you Mrs Pritchard, had a nasty cold early autumn but she's getting better now.'

'That's good then; just that she didn't come to the chapel sewing group for the poor people in Lancashire and I was just wondering, hoping everything was okay with her. My cousin's boy, Jonathan, very observant him, he remembered seeing her at last spring's horse fair in Carmarthen but not seen her since.'

'Well she's fine like I say, thank you Mrs Pritchard,' said Nest turning away with measured finality.

That evening after they'd eaten, Nest told Siôn about her conversation with Alys Pritchard. Siôn was the same calm man as always.

'It was bound to happen sooner or later.'

'But that doesn't make it any easier to deal with Siôn.'

'No but we'll just do what we said we do, keep Caroline busy indoors and carry on our lives as usual.' Nest nodded, deep in thought as her husband continued. 'I do think we should be seeing about Mrs Goodbody though,' he said speaking of the person whose name they'd been given by the doctor. 'She'll need some notice and we must make sure she's got a room for Caroline when she needs it. I assume you still think is the best thing to do?'

'No doubt about that. There's no way we could keep it a secret if she had the *baban* here.'

'How long do you think we could afford to keep her with Mrs Goodbody before the birth?'

'I don't know, three or four weeks I'd hope. Next time you're going to Carmarthen, I'll come with you and go and see her,' said Nest.

In Carmarthen they found Mrs Goodbody's reputation as a kind and non–judgmental soul to be well-founded and manifest in her manner and clothes, a sober, dark green dress with a pale yellow blouse set off with a bow in green to match her dress. Nest felt she'd found in Mrs Goodbody a practical businesswoman as well as an understanding and realistic lady. Nest agreed that Caroline should move to Mrs Goodbody's home in Goose Street, near the centre of Carmarthen a month before her baby was expected and for her to help earn part of her keep doing dressmaking and other light chores around the house. Nest explained to Mrs Goodbody the story she and Siôn proposed to tell people when the baby went back to their farm and again Mrs Goodbody's experience helped.

'Leave the *baban* with me and have Caroline back at home

12

for a few weeks after the birth. I'm sure I'll know a girl who'll wet-nurse the *baban*. Make sure your Caroline's seen around the village acting as normal. That will stop most of the gossips and allow you to put around the story about your husband's relative up in Machynlleth.'

'I hope we're doing the right thing,' said Nest.

'Who knows? said Mrs Goodbody, 'but if you want other people to believe the story it's important you believe it yourselves.' Nest clenched her hands.

'It's just that I don't know what I'll say if someone challenges me,' she sighed.

'Who's the most likely to do that?' asked Mrs Goodbody.

'Alys Pritchard, the wretched preacher's wife, for one. Not only does she behave like she's God's elect but like all preachers and their families, they travel around and their wives gossip everywhere they go.'

'I know the woman,' nodded Mrs Goodbody. 'Thinks far too much of herself.'

'Their husbands preach forgiveness and love and understanding but in reality I think they're the biggest hypocrites around.'

'And that's the truth, I'm sure, but us fretting about it won't stop them so leave it be. Let's not bother ourselves about the things we can't change and get busy with those we can, and Lord knows there's enough of them Mrs Lewis.'

'You're right Mrs Goodbody. *Diolch yn fawr.* You're a great comfort.'

'Think nothing of it. Caroline isn't the first girl I've taken care of and she won't be the last. Now you get home and take care of your daughter and I'll get on with the girls I have here now.'

In the event Caroline was well into the last month of her pregnancy the evening Siôn and Nest put her carefully into their trap and drove her slowly to Mrs Goodbody's home in Carmarthen. A cold easterly wind, presaging a grim winter to come, picked up as they left and

Caroline pulled the thick woollen coat her mother had bought her for the winter close around her and tucked her scarf in around the neck. Aware that childbirth was as risky for the mother as for the child, Nest bade an emotional farewell to her daughter. As ever, Mrs Goodbody was reassuring and practical.

'Come and see her whenever you want, no need to send word,' she said to Nest and Siôn.

'Thank you Mrs Goodbody, I will,' replied Nest.

'You too Mr Lewis. Whenever you're in town. It's not just her mother a girl needs at times like these. Now, off home to your boys. You two put your trust in me and in the Lord. I can't promise anything but together we've not done too badly till now,' said Mrs Goodbody busily. The women embraced, Siôn shook Mrs Goodbody's hand and together man and wife rode home in thoughtful silence.

Chapter 2: Amelia

As old wives tales often tell, Caroline's first baby was later than expected and by the time Mrs Goodbody's note reached Newchurch, Nest and Siôn had started to fear the worst for their daughter. Amelia, the name Caroline had already decided upon if her baby was a girl, was born on Wednesday, 17th March 1847, a bright, dry day in South Wales under a sky of high, light clouds. Mrs Goodbody had made sure the birth had been registered in Carmarthen within a few days of her birth. Like many people at the time Caroline had never learnt to read or write and it was Mrs Goodbody who helped her complete the formal documents. As soon as Caroline was strong enough to travel, Siôn and Nest came to drive her back to the farm, again under cover of darkness. Once she was settled her mother ensured she was seen by as many of the village people as possible in the days that followed. A chapel knitting circle, Mrs Pritchard's latest enthusiasm, had just started and Caroline, always a competent and gifted craftswoman, made an early appearance and threw herself into the group's work with gusto and endeavour. Seeing she was clearly without a child and in good health contradicted the insinuations Mrs Pritchard had been circulating in the previous weeks and the welcome the pastor's wife gave Caroline was contrived and graceless.

A month or so later, as she and Siôn had planned, Nest gathered a group of "friends" who she could rely on to gossip her "secret news".

'We've had terrible shock,' she said. The friends, always keen to hear someone else's bad news made appropriate sympathetic noises. 'A cousin of my Siôn's in Machynlleth passed away having her baby six weeks or so ago.'

'Oh dear how sad. Was she old? I do hope it wasn't painful,' and so on the usual platitudes tumbled out.

'Tragic really.' The sympathies intensified. 'She's only been married a couple of years, and the baby was her first.'

'In childbirth too? Oh how tragic. Was the *baban* dead too?'

'No the baby, a beautiful girl was saved,' continued Nest.

'Terrible burden for her father then?'

'Worse even. He's almost 48 himself. No sisters, no family at all, so no chance of bringing up the daughter alone.'

'How sad is that. Awful position to be in,' the usual sympathetic platitudes continued.

'Well lucky we heard because Siôn and I decided we couldn't see the little innocent one suffer so we're going to adopt her,' Nest announced quietly and without ceremony or fanfare. There was a brief silence as the news was absorbed by the gathered women. 'Of course, I'm mentioning this in confidence mind. I know I can trust your discretion.' Nods and murmurs of assent all round.

'My, that'll be a big responsibility for you both,' said some while others wondered 'how will Siôn cope with the new *baban* keeping him awake at night?' In answer to all the questions Nest quietly reminded them that 'she and Siôn had already brought up four children and that one more dear little girl wouldn't present them with a problem.'

Naturally Mrs Pritchard smirked knowingly when the news reached her and commented acidly to her closest gossips that 'hadn't she said almost exactly the same thing all along,' and 'there's no smoke without fire–you know what I mean.'

Nevertheless, and as Mrs Goodbody had predicted, because Nest and her family steadfastly maintained their own story, the doubters and gossips were left with only their own doubts and tittle-tattle to convey and ultimately most people in the village lost interest in their malicious stories.

Away from the farm Nest did her best to ensure that baby Amelia was seen with her as she shopped and carried on her usual life but once indoors, just as Nest and Siôn had impressed upon Caroline from the start, most of the burden fell on the baby's real mother. As the family had foreseen, when Amelia started to talk she learnt to call Caroline 'Mam' and Nest 'Nain' but when uttered in company this was dismissed as a child's confusion with Siôn's mid-Wales accent. It was an implausible explanation but served to satisfy all but the most cynical of Mrs Pritchard's friends.

Less simple to explain convincingly was the baby's slightly auburn hair that contrasted vividly with Nest and Siôn's typically Celtic dark hair and dark eyes that they'd passed on to their natural children. When pressed to comment the family explained that the old man, Amelia's 'natural' father in Machynlleth, had originally come over from Ulster. Like her calling Caroline 'Mam' this explanation failed to persuade Mrs Pritchard's group, but then as Siôn continued to remind the family, even if the Archangel Gabriel had appeared to assure Mrs Pritchard they were telling the truth, the preacher's wife and her friends would have accused even God's messenger of being mistaken.

For most people in the village the plausibility of the family's subterfuge was greatly aided by the steadfast maintenance of the detail by Nest and Siôn's sons. Despite Siôn's early doubts about Oswain's reliability, once Amelia began to walk she seemed to form a happy bond with her 'adopted' middle brother. A more uncomplaining, amenable and loving child it would have been hard to imagine and within a few years these characteristics more than any others led to her complete acceptance as an integral part of the family. Pastor and Mrs Pritchard had moved on to a circuit in the north of Wales and Amelia attended Sunday school regularly, learnt her prayers and acquired an innate politeness that villagers always commented favourably upon.

'She's such a happy little girl, Mam,' remarked Caroline to her mother one summer afternoon as they watched Amelia playing with a couple of baby rabbits Oswain had brought to show the child.
'She's easy to please and Oswain and Daniel adore her.'
'I'm pleased about that. I was concerned they'd never properly

accept her as part of the family,' said Caroline.

'No, she's such a loveable little girl. I'm not surprised the boys fell for her, an' you've done a good job teaching her manners. People always remark on it.'

'I had a good teacher Mam,' said Caroline smiling at her mother and reaching to squeeze her forearm.

'Worries me though Caroline,' said her mother suddenly more seriously.

'What does?' questioned Caroline.

'What's going to happen if you get married. People think your Dada and I adopted her, but you'd want to take her with your husband I assume.'

'Well I'm not aware of any potential husbands lurking in the bushes, so I don't think that's something that's going to bother us any time soon,' replied her daughter confidently. 'Plus it'd need to be a special man to take me and a baby!'

'But it's likely going to happen sometime, my girl.'

'Well we'll deal with that when the time comes. Until then don't let's spoil the family.'

Sadly, the Wheel of Fortune that had played such a dominant role in the minds and imaginations of people since medieval times, revolved and imposed its own sad solution on Nest and Siôn's family. Although outbreaks of serious diseases like tuberculosis, cholera and even the plague had caused large-scale deaths in urban communities in Britain since the 14th century, in Wales there were sporadic localised infections even as late as the 19th century. One such occurred in Presteigne while Rhys, now mature enough to do an adult's job on the farm, was in the border town negotiating to buy a new herd of sheep. Within days of his return to Newchurch he'd fallen ill and been diagnosed with plague. The principal burden of nursing him had fallen on Caroline and in her care Rhys recovered. Tragically, after a bitter and determined fight, Caroline herself succumbed to the disease and died aged only 28. Amelia, was as distraught as any child of 6 could be at losing her mother and as a result inevitably turned to Nest for her comfort and love. For Nest soothing the child's need was both cathartic and gently easing as they shared their grief. As Nest recalled years later it was the moment she probably bonded more closely with Amelia than she ever had with Caroline and she devoted the rest of her life to the little infant. Eventually Nest instilled in Amelia her own love of books and reading.

Education and the need for children to be taught to read, write and count had been a topic of disagreement between Siôn and Nest from the time they first met. Although neither of them had any formal education, Nest had listened carefully to the Nonconformist preachers who'd been active in Wales for a century or more by then and whose Sunday schools she'd attended. There she'd learnt to read and by the time she married her reading and writing were well up to standard for the day. Siôn, on the other hand had been put to work on the family's farm almost as soon as he could walk. Inevitably their views were conditioned by their individual experiences.

'Reading's OK for preachers and teachers but farmers don't need it, Nest,' was Siôn's view. 'Long as a farmer can add and count so he knows he's not being cheated, that's enough. What else does he want learning for?'

'If'n you can't read how do you know what's in the contracts you have to agree?' asked his wife.

'I only deal with men I can trust. My mark's good enough for any contract and a handshake's good enough a seal for the law, you know that.'

'And how about improving yourself?'

'When I've got enough money for luxuries like books, I'll worry about improving myself, anyway, aren't I interesting enough for you like I am?' he smiled warmly enough to defuse the situation and avoid any argument.

'Course you are you lovely man, I'm not complaining, you know that.'

'Then we'll hear no more about book learning then,' Siôn said with finality.

Unfortunately, Siôn's intransigence and the family's lack of money meant that as their children grew none of them could read, write or count beyond the basics. Now, 20 years on and unexpectedly faced with Amelia's new, young mind in their family Nest persuaded Siôn to let her teach Amelia all she could. Since their family finances weren't as limited as they had been before, Siôn was hard put to deny his wife's wishes.

The subsequent ten years brought big changes to Siôn's family. As Siôn himself began to retire from the daily grind on the farm, Rhys became the *de facto* head of the business. Daniel realised that most of the farms in the area could only sustain a certain size of family. Instead of staying at home he took forestry work near Rhayader and moved to mid-Wales a couple of years after Caroline died. Oswain too left the farm and joined the crew of a ship sailing out of Burry Port near Llanelli even though his departure left Amelia inconsolable for weeks. In his retirement Siôn found what was for him a surprising but absorbing interest in philately. Initially he was inspired by the letters Oswain wrote from the various ports he visited around the world and which Amelia read aloud to the family as they sat around the kitchen table after their evening meals.

On his 35th birthday Rhys took over the tenancy of the farm from his father. A year later, during one of the severest winters anyone could remember, his father insisted on helping get their sheep to shelter. The declining demand for farm goods meant the farm was cold and damp and the chill that Siôn caught after spending too long helping his son in the cold worsened to pneumonia over the Christmas period. Before the following spring brought warmer, dry weather he breathed his last leaving a helpless and sorrowing family.

With her ageing grandmother constantly grieving for her husband, Amelia, now 17, was fully employed helping her uncle run the farm.

Despite immense goodwill and love in the family, Nest was acutely aware that the situation could not be sustained for ever. Indeed, shortly after his father's death and without telling his mother, Rhys met Ceinwen, a widow visiting her brother, a friend of Rhys' in Newcastle Emlyn to the west of Newchurch. Ceinwen's husband, Harri, a farmer from Pembrokeshire, had died in an accident on a farm machine. Blue-eyed, lively and blessed with a slim figure, delicate features and beautiful, soft skin, Ceinwen had fallen for Rhys almost as soon as they met. During several visits Ceinwen made to see her brother she and Rhys fell in love and they resolved to tell Rhys' mother as soon as they felt she could bear the news following her husband's death. When they did, although she was privately a little disappointed that her son had been meeting Ceinwen behind her back, she understood why and welcomed the girl with genuine affection. Ceinwen had told Nest how she'd inherited the farm she and Harri had owned and Nest understood that Rhys was torn between his responsibility to his family and the farm they'd rented for three generations in Newchurch and his desire to marry Ceinwen and move to Pembrokeshire and their own property.

'You've got your own life to lead Rhys,' Nest reassured him. 'I can get some help to run this place and Amelia's here to help as well. We'll manage.'

'I don't want you to just manage, Mam. You deserve more, plus you took on the responsibility for bringing up Amelia which wasn't a choice you and Dada made.'

'Don't blame Amelia, lad,' said Nest sternly. 'She may not have been what I expected from life but I wouldn't have it any other way. She means as much to me as any of my own children, so we'll have no more of that talk. Not now and not ever.'

The solution to the problem that Nest and Rhys felt they had about their separate and individual futures finally appeared almost out of the blue one summer evening. Rhys and Ceinwen, with whom he was now deeply in love, were strolling on the hill above her farm in Pembrokeshire discussing a problem they were facing.

'I really don't know why you're fretting about this Rhys, surely the answer is in our own hands?'

'How's that *cariad*? I don't understand,' he said.

'Look, I realise that when we're married you want us to have our own farm,' she said.

'Of course,' Rhys replied, 'any farmer would.'

'But surely *fy caru* it doesn't have to be *this* farm?' asked Ceinwen.

'I assumed that was a given,' he paused. 'Are you suggesting we should sell your farm?'

'Why not? It's just a farm that I came to live in when I married Harri. Other than that the place has no emotional ties for me. They passed away with my husband. He was a good man, you know that, I've told you already, but he's not here any more. Now I want to marry you, be part of your family so why don't we sell this farm and buy another farm near yours in Newchurch? It could be big enough to support your mother and your sister as long as they wanted to live there and in the long term provide us with a sound investment to pass on to our family. You do want to have children with me don't you?' she said slipping her hand into his and, turning her head towards him, kissed him passionately on the lips. As their kiss ended Rhys sat back, smiling silently at Ceinwen, absorbing all the ramifications of what she'd just proposed. Finally, as the sinking sun flickered its last red beams across Ceinwen's face Rhys said, 'Well, that was quite a speech. Have you been practicing?'

'I'll say this for your Ceinwen,' said Nest to her son, 'she's a brave girl.'

'Why's she brave Mam? There's many who say I'm the brave one taking on another man's widow.'

'True,' said Nest, 'but what I mean is that a young widow marrying a second husband and moving to another county is one thing, but having your mother-in-law and a young niece come to live with you as well–or is that a niece-in-law?' she teased him, 'well that's another thing altogether.'

In fact, for the most part Nest's fears were resolved at their first meeting when Ceinwen came to Newchurch to meet Rhys' family. When she judged the moment was right and she wouldn't be thought too pushy, Ceinwen put forward her suggestion about buying a farm for them all to live in. Nest was pleased to discover that having come from her parents' home to marry her first husband Ceinwen had already learned to appreciate other people's idiosyncrasies and understand their concerns. Over three days and long evenings the four of them had discussed the pros and cons of Ceinwen's suggestions. At the end of the three days the idea had been agreed and the decision made. Almost at once Nest threw herself into the task of finding a suitable farm in the area around Newchurch and Ceinwen put her property in Pembrokeshire in the hands of a reputable agent in the county town. By the end of her visit Nest had found a 350-acre farm high on the hills outside Newchurch. The land was well-drained, a mixture of arable and sheep and, most important of all, had been consistently profitable. The previous owner had died and the sale was being handled by an agent for the owner's son who'd emigrated to Australia and wasn't keen to return to Wales. This meant the seller wasn't influenced by any other farming considerations but was concerned solely with getting the best price in the quickest time.

Unfortunately Ceinwen encountered in Pembrokeshire the general depression in farm prices, particularly those further away from the fast-growing coalfields in the Glamorgan valleys north of Cardiff. As autumn approached and the days grew shorter Ceinwen and Rhys became increasingly disconsolate and depressed that they'd received so few serious offers for Ceinwen's farm.

'Look *cariad*, we both agreed that the farm at Newchurch is exactly right for us but if we can't sell this place and especially if we can't get the price we've told the agent we need, we may have to ask your mother and Amelia to come and live here in Pembrokeshire,' said Ceinwen.

'I understand that Ceinwen, and this farm might support the

two of us, but not my mother and Amelia as well.'

'Maybe Amelia would give up her plans to go to college and work with us on the farm?' suggested Ceinwen cautiously.

'She's got her heart set on being a teacher *cariad*. I really don't want to disappoint her unless it's absolutely necessary,' said Rhys. 'I'll write to the agent handling Newchurch and see if I can persuade him to give us a little more time.'

'I agree. Something will turn up,' said Ceinwen hopefully.

And it did. Evidently the seller in Australia found he needed money urgently and cabled to his agent saying he'd accept a slightly lower offer on the farm at Newchurch. At almost the same time a firm from Aberdare making pit props for the coalmines in the Taff and Rhondda valleys discovered the ideal wood they needed in the copse on Ceinwen's Pembrokeshire farm. The agent, a resourceful and imaginative man arranged for the outright sale of the wood in the copse and a long-term tenancy of the farm. Within six weeks the contracts for the sale of the trees and the lease of Ceinwen's farm had been finalised and Rhys and Nest had given notice to quit their tenancy. Their landlord's agent hadn't been happy with the short notice they'd given him but he'd finally accepted that not only was there was no point in arguing but he had another tenant waiting to take over the farm. A month later Rhys and Ceinwen were married in a quiet ceremony at Carmarthen Registry Office witnessed by Nest, Amelia and just their closest friends and the whole new family moved into the new farm.

Very late one evening, just a few days after the family moved in there was a brisk knocking on the front door. A severe storm earlier in the evening had made it difficult to keep the lamps burning steadily and everyone had gone to bed. That caused a short delay until Rhys was able to open the door. At first he didn't recognise the bearded, wet and rather bedraggled man waiting outside.

'Can I help you?' he asked the caller.

'I would say it's any port in a storm but you'd probably not understand,' the man said turning to Rhys.

'*Duw*! It's Oswain! Come inside boy, and get those wet things off,' he turned from the door and shouted upstairs. 'Mam! Ceinwen, Milly! It's Oswain!' Then turning to his brother again,' My you've put on a bit of weight there boy.'

'Solid muscle mind.'

'Well solid anyway,' laughed the boys.

A rushing of feet resounded through the farmhouse as shoes were slipped on and cloaks were flung around shoulders. First to appear was Ceinwen, her hair still in night curls.

'*Cariad,* this is Oswain, my brother,' then turning to Oswain, 'this is my wife, Ceinwen.' Oswain leaned towards her, took her hand and kissed it gently though the stubble of his beard tickled her.

'Pretty lady you got there boy,' he said without taking his eyes off Ceinwen.

'And what a gent you are, brother,' she replied. 'I can see the likeness though your eyes are blue and your hair is curlier than Rhys'. Welcome anyway.'

'And how did you know where to find us Oswain? We've not been here a week yet,' asked Rhys.

'That I know for sure. I've been lugging this bag halfway round the county looking for you,' replied Oswain. 'Left my big trunk at the station in Carmarthen...'

He stopped as just then Amelia emerged, her hair brushed through and falling around her shoulders.

'Hello Oswain,' she said softly.

'Amelia, you've grown. You're lovely,' said Oswain glowing with fraternal love and pride. He stepped forward to kiss her, lingering in his embrace.

'Stop it you're embarrassing me, here I'll make some tea.'

'I think he might prefer a beer, no?' asked Rhys.

'Maybe later, right now tea sounds very good. Strong and just a bit of milk please. And where's Mam? She alright?'

'She's very alright, my son,' said Nest pushing the door a little wider so she could walk in.

'Let me look at you Oswain *bach*. My how you've grown. You must be six inches taller than your brother here. Can't call him big brother no more can we?'

'Hello Mam. I've missed you something awful,' said Oswain hugging his mother close.

'Well you're home safe so my prayers have been answered. Now sit you down for goodness sake. You want something to eat? I've got some roast beef from Sunday so it's quite fresh. Could make you a sandwich *bach*.'

'No I'm fine Mam, just pleased to see you all again.'

'Well some tea if you please Amelia *fy caru*, just tell us all your news,' encouraged Nest.

'It could take a while mind.'

'Then we've got all the time in the world my son,' she said squeezing his hand.

The family talked long into the night though none of them wanted to sleep. Stories of their lives since they were last together tumbled out in loose disarray and only paused as the sky lightened and the new morning dawned. Next day, much though they all wanted to continue the recounting of their lives since Oswain had gone to sea, work on the farm had to continue. Very soon the rhythm of a new routine took over; Oswain joined in the family's work around the farm during the day and in the evening after they'd cleared the supper dishes away they gathered round to exchange news and retell events many of which had been almost forgotten.

'So let me get this clear Oswain,' said Rhys a few evenings later, 'after you left Burry Port you first went to South America? That right?'

'Not strictly. I went first on a coaster down to Swansea. It was there I signed on to the big schooner bound for South America, Patagonia actually.'

'And that's in Argentina, right?'

'Yes but before we got there we stopped at a load of ports

from Trinidad in the Caribbean, British Guiana–that's on the mainland of South America–we took on a load of sugar there, right down the coast of Brazil. Man that's a long way. Brazil goes on forever.'

'Did you see cannibals?' asked Ceinwen.

'Might have done but we didn't get near enough to find out if they'd rather have eaten us than salt beef,' laughed Oswain.

'So what comes after Brazil, Patagonia?' asked Rhys.

'*Duw,* no there's hundreds of miles away but while we were still off Brazil we did cross the Equator.'

'What did that feel like?' said Nest. Oswain smiled, unsure whether his mother's question was serious because of her lack of schooling or if she was joking.

'The old sea dogs said we'd feel a bump but in truth there was so much grog–that's rum–flowing that day in a sort of celebration, I can't remember if I felt a bump or not.'

'So what you mean boy,' said Rhys lapsing into the terms they used as kids, 'is there's no difference on the other side of the Equator?'

'Of course not, though after we got much further south it was odd to look in the sky and see the sun to the north of us. All our lives here the sun's in the south isn't it? Takes a bit of getting used to seeing it in the north.'

And so the evening progressed until it was almost time for the men to go to bed and Nest, who'd listened to the conversation in silence for most of the time, just watching her sons, interjected her own question.

'So Oswain, before I fall asleep, tell me about Patagonia. Is it true it's full of Welsh?'

'I don't think I'd say "full" but in one province there's so many people speaking Welsh–or something that sounds like it anyway–you'd think you were at home–well up north perhaps.'

'So do they have mines and slag tips and stuff or are they all farmers like us?' asked Ceinwen.

27

'There's no mines as far I know. Remember it's some way from the coast but my impression was that they're all cowboys, herding cattle and sheep.'

'Well I never,' marvelled Nest. 'Whatever's the world coming to, Welsh cowboys. Right off to bed, *nos da* you all.'

'Just before you go Oswain,' said Rhys, 'did you sail round Cape Horn?'

'Why yes, several times,' replied his brother.

'And was it as dangerous and fearful as they say?'

'Depends on the weather how dangerous it really is but it's where the two oceans meet sort of, the Pacific and the Atlantic and they collide a bit with each other. The worst time was...'

'He'll tell you tomorrow Rhys *bach*,' interrupted Ceinwen. 'Now, bed boy.'

'But I forget what I want to ask him *cariad*.'

'Then it's probably untrue *bach*. Now bed.'

Oswain's telling of his experiences around South America and in the South Seas was interrupted a few days later when his younger brother, Daniel arrived at the farm. Built much like his older brother, Daniel was lithe and slim. Neither he nor Rhys had acquired Oswain's bulk. Nest had asked Amelia to write to him shortly after Oswain had arrived and he'd taken some time off from his job in Rhayader. Nest made sure her youngest son, who was still wearing the leather trousers and hunting jacket he wore at work, was as welcome and as comfortable as the rest of her family. It was grand she thought to have her sons back under her roof again and even if Caroline wasn't there at least Amelia was. Of course the round of storytelling and catching-up started over again, this time including Daniel's life working in the forests around mid-Wales. Compared to Oswain's tales, Daniel's life was more mundane but he was no less anxious than the others to hear about Oswain's adventures.

'So tell me Oswain,' said Daniel, 'did you get to America, I mean the United States?'

'Of course, Danny–you sure you want me to call you Danny?'

28

'It's what they all call me at work but whatever you like's alright with me.'

'I don't suppose you're asking me,' said Nest, 'but Daniel is what your father and I named you and I still like it, but I suppose it's very modern to have a short name so, carry on eh? Tell us about America then.'

'I'd say the cities are pretty much what I expected, big, noisy, tough and soulless. No community, no sense of belonging other than to gangs. On the other hand outside the cities you could be anywhere. Very big of course, but otherwise much like country life here. Biggest difference is the darkies. Everyone there told us that they are going to be America's biggest problem and no answers in sight.'

'Were you ever in port long enough to get to know any of the locals?' said Daniel.

'Thanks to our First Mate we nearly got an extended stay in California, guests of the police,' replied Oswain.

'Arrested you mean?' exclaimed Rhys.

'Exactly.'

'*Duw*,' said Nest with an intake of breath. 'What on earth did you do to get arrested?'

'It wasn't what I or most of the crew did. While we were docked in San Francisco the First Mate and a couple of the crew decided to do a bit of personal shipping.'

'What? Gold? Currency?' guessed Daniel.

'No, guns, to be precise Winchester repeater rifles, those that don't have to be reloaded after every shot.'

'Why do they need rifles on a ship?'

'They didn't want them for themselves, they were going to sell them.'

'It's very puzzling to me,' said Nest rising from the table to make a pot of tea.

'They made a deal to buy them from gangsters in San Francisco and to deliver them to Mexican rebels in small ports down the Mexican coast. The rebels who are fighting the government were

29

desperate to get their hands on modern guns and paid very handsomely. Trouble was the US government is very good at discovering secrets and when the First Mate and his pals started to stow the rifles late one night well you'd have thought the whole US army had turned out. There were policemen everywhere.'

'What happened to the First Mate and his friends?' asked Nest.

'They got long prison sentences and when they've served those sentences in jail they'll be expelled from the USA for ever.'

'Thank goodness the police believed the rest of the crew were not involved,' said Ceinwen.

'They didn't at first and for a while we were all under suspicion. The owners were furious and sent word to their agent in San Francisco threatening to sack us all. The police couldn't believe that only three men could organise such a huge smuggling operation but that's what it really was.'

'Thank goodness I brought up honest boys,' said Nest.

'I agree Mam, though I have to say that after we'd sailed there were stories and gossip about the master, that's the captain, being in collusion with the authorities and getting a reward,' said Oswain.

'I'm just glad you had the good sense to stay out of trouble boy,' said Nest gathering the dishes in front of her and taking them to the sink.

Before Daniel and Oswain had discussed their plans with the others the restored domesticity of her home had persuaded Nest to think or at least to hope that all her family would then stay in the general area so she could spend her old age with her kin all round her. Her hopes began to fade after tea one evening a few weeks later when Daniel was telling the family about his life.

'Trouble is you see, the government is worried about the power the big landowners like my boss have over what they now call "natural resources"–what we used to call trees and lakes and things.'

'Pity they didn't get interested in more than money when the landowners decided to dig out the coal,' said Rhys ruefully. 'Might

30

have saved a good few lives underground and prevented our valleys being stuffed full of cheap houses and them threatened by huge slag tips.'

'I never understood why they didn't use the slag to keep the galleries safe and not use props all the time,' said Ceinwen.

'Money isn't it,' said Oswain bitterly. 'They'd have to pay the men to mix the slag with cement or whatever and take it back underground. No profit in that. Much cheaper to buy a few lengths of cable and dump the slag on the hills they already own.'

'Mark my words *bach*,' said Rhys, 'that's one decision the owners will come to regret. One day those black piles will bite back. Anyway Danny, what they planning to do with the trees?'

'There's talk about some sort of committee or council with the power to control what the landowners do with their forests and woodland.'

'You mean tell the owners what they can and can't do with their own land?' asked Rhys quite surprised.

'Exactly that.'

'Don't sound so bad to me,' shrugged Ceinwen, 'not if it saves men's lives and stops the owners ruining the views just to make money.'

'I agree, in principle anyway,' nodded Daniel, 'but you know what happens when you give a group of men control over something as big as forests or farming, next thing they'll be making other decisions way outside what was originally planned for them.'

'Danny lad, seems to me you're siding with the landowners. You had a conversion on your road to Damascus?' asked Oswain

'And that'll be enough of taking the word of the Lord in vain, thank you,' interjected Nest.

'Sorry Mam but just saying how Danny sounded like he was on the bosses' side.'

'It's not always a matter of sides Oswain,' said Daniel sitting forward and spreading his hands on the table. 'Trees are living things. They take years to grow. Some of the trees where I'm working were saplings before our grandfather was born. My boss

31

only allows me to cut down certain trees. He calls it selectivity or something. Basically it means we thin out the forest, cutting down some trees and leaving others. Then we plant new saplings in the spaces so that in years to come there'll be trees ready to fell but others still growing to maturity. And that means the views are kept looking much as they've always looked.'

'Surely it's easier to just cut down the whole of one part of the forest completely and then re-plant over the clear ground. Stands to reason it'll cost less too,' commented Oswain.

'And that might be what a government department would decide, but it shouldn't always be about money.

'Tell that to the mine-owners,' said Rhys wearily.

'In the end money talks; always did, always will,' said Oswain with conviction, 'at least until we change the way we're governed.'

'Perhaps,' nodded Daniel, 'and if this government commission they're talking about concerns itself only with stopping the greedy landowners that'll be fine. What I fear is that they'll go further and start deciding where people can build houses, how many houses can be built, where the roads will go, even what size the farms will be. The land isn't a single entity. It's a mixture and combination of fields, farms, animals, trees, rivers, and, of course people, and the wise landowners think about them all. I don't see a government panel doing that.'

'So what would you do, Danny?' asked Ceinwen.

'I don't know, me,' sighed Daniel. 'I'm thinking about going to New Zealand maybe.' The colour drained from Nest's face as she turned sharply to her son.

'What's New Zealand got that Wales hasn't *bach*?' she queried.

'According to what I've found out New Zealand's like a huge version of Wales, at least Wales like it used to be. Clean air, clear water...'

'...low wages, poor housing, hard labour all dependent on the weather or the landlord. If that's New Zealand, you can keep it boy,'

32

interrupted Oswain angrily.

'Now, now boys, no arguments round my table please,' begged Nest. 'Disagree, but no arguments.' Then, turning to Daniel, 'and when might you be going to New Zealand?'

'Oh I don't know Mam, no rush. I'll give you plenty of notice.'

'That's good then. I'm getting too old for nasty surprises.'

In the end, after many more evenings spent reminiscing and remembering days long gone, the family didn't stay together or even nearby. The travelling bug had bitten Oswain and he signed up with a company whose ships sailed all over the world from Bristol. The whole family went to the station to see him off. Nest wore a new blue coat the boys had clubbed together to buy her as a parting gift. The broad collar was adorned with a real fox fur "all the latest fashion, and guaranteed to keep you warm around the neck" as Ceinwen described it.

For some years Oswain continued to write brief letters to his mother as he had to his father. Sadly they were badly spelt and revealed the lack of basic education he'd had while he was growing up. Nest, and later Rhys, continued to collect the stamps from his letters. Then, after almost a year had passed without any letters arriving, Rhys received a formal notification from the shipping company informing him that his brother's ship had foundered in a typhoon in the South China Sea. All hands were lost said the document and asked Rhys to confirm that the address and details were correct. Following his affirmation that Oswain's mother, named as his next of kin, was still alive the company sent Nest Oswain's outstanding pay and benefits.

Shortly after Oswain left for Bristol, Daniel went back to Rhayader, gave his notice and served out his time. His boss, Lord Cadwalladr, invited him to lunch shortly before he left, a rare honour, especially considering that the owner wasn't always in Wales.

'We shall miss you Daniel, you've been a rare asset to the estate,' he said over a large round glass half full of French cognac.

'It's been a pleasure working on the estate these past years, sir. I've learnt a great deal since I arrived,' he replied.

'What you've learnt is a credit to you for you were a good pupil. Old Watkins had been head forester for my father and frankly I was very concerned about finding someone who could fill his boots when he retired. It was a gamble taking you on I'll admit but I felt you had something about you and I decided to take a risk.'

'I'm glad you did, sir, for I learned a great deal from Mr Watkins. I'd be lying if I said I wasn't going to miss the job and the other staff on the estate,' said Daniel.

'Well Daniel, notwithstanding my regret at losing you I understand the concern you have about the woodland on the estate and the changes the government is talking about bringing in. It amazes me that there are still owners–people with much bigger estates than this one–who don't see the wisdom in our approach and still insist on putting profit above everything else.'

'But isn't it the same with everything sir?'

'What do you mean Daniel?'

'It seems to me that in almost every enterprise there are some, often only a few, who ignore the long-term benefit of what they're involved with and think only of short-term profit. There's always some whether it's railway companies, coal mines, spinners, weavers or ship-owners who'll take the easy, short-sighted way.'

'And don't you think you'll find the same in New Zealand?' asked Lord Cadwalladr.

'Probably will sir, but I'm told there's a scheme for new arrivals to acquire their own land and, in the long term to pass it on without the pressures to break up estates like people had to under the old Welsh laws.'

'I hope that's true though of course English law has never had that nonsense. Anyway, drink up. I've got an appointment with my lawyer ironically,' he laughed. As they shook hands Lord Cadwalladr handed Daniel a sealed envelope.

'Open this later. It's just a token of my gratitude and my very best wishes for your future.'

34

Later, in the privacy of his room Daniel found a bank draft payable to him for £100. He wrote a note of thanks immediately.

Eventually, it came time for Daniel to leave for New Zealand. He came to Newchurch to say farewell to his mother and family. Nest watched him leave with tears in her eyes as Rhys drove his brother in their trap to catch the train in Carmarthen. Despite the hopes and best intentions mother and both her younger sons expressed, the ache in her heart as she watched them leave told her she would never see either of them again.

Six months after landing in New Zealand Daniel had purchased land with the capital given him by Lord Cadwalladr and started breeding hardy strains of Welsh sheep suited to the harsh conditions of their environment. The scale of the farms was huge. Careful husbandry of his farm and capital along the prudent business lines he'd promoted in Rhayader led eventually to an enterprise of over 5,000 acres. In between he married Delyth, a New Zealander whose parents, like Daniel, had emigrated from Wales. They had two sons both of whom volunteered and fought in the fledgling New Zealand army when it first fought overseas in WW1. Tragically both boys were killed at Gallipoli and their names are engraved on the Chunuk Bair memorial to the New Zealanders who died fighting for Britain.

Chapter 3: Griffith, Rhys and Ceinwen

Griffith Thomas was born at the farm his family had rented for more than 60 years in Cynwyl Elfed, a small village a few miles north of the county town amid the rolling hills of Carmarthenshire. Tall, strong and with a mop of curly, dark-brown hair, he'd worked full-time with his father and his uncle on the farm since he was 12. The exclusively masculine environment on the farm was a constant topic of conversation amongst other villagers even though it had come about as a result of a series of tragedies rather than by design or choice.

Griffith's father's brother, Uncle Aron, had been married briefly. The couple had lived in Fishguard where he'd taken a job on ships working the Welsh and Irish coasts. During a particularly severe spring storm his wife had been waiting on the dock for his return when a freak wave caught her, swept her out to sea and she drowned. Emrys, Griffith's father, insisted Aron join him and his wife, Lowri, at the farm in Cynwyl. Sadly, yet more tragedy befell the family when Lowri was giving birth to their second child. Complications arose and Lowri and the baby perished within three hours of each other.

Emrys, Aron and Griffith led a uniquely male though hardly monastic life. Their reputation for drinking and carousing with loose women from Carmarthen caused most of the Cynwyl Elfed mothers to ensure their daughters stayed clear of the men and their farm. Needless to say, the stories and the men's reputations, often exaggerated by the retelling, were as fascinating for the young women of the area as they were cautionary.

As if to contradict stories of the men's licentious living and drunkenness Griffith and Emrys were regular worshippers each Sunday at the Baptist Chapel in Cynwyl Elfed. Griffith's warm, brown baritone voice in particular was much appreciated.

The chapel at Cynwyl happened to be the nearest Baptist chapel to Newchurch and the remote location of the Lewis' new farm meant that Nest could only attend worship when one of the family could drive her there in the trap. When she joined the chapel choir Amelia who would usually walk to the chapel inevitably caught Griffith's eye. After the third weekly Saturday evening practice he persuaded her not to set off on the long walk home alone in the gathering gloom but allow him to accompany her even though he then had to walk all the way back again. Had Rhys been a few minutes earlier in walking towards the village that evening he'd have bumped into Griffith chatting flirtatiously with his niece about half a mile from their home.

'I'm sorry I'm late *cariad*,' said Rhys out of breath from hurrying up the hill.

'Don't worry, Rhys,' Amelia assured her uncle, 'one of the men from the choir walked most of the way with me.'

'Ah, that's good then. Who was it, anyone I'd know?'

'Griffith Thomas, one of the baritones in the choir, y'know, the one with the curly hair.'

'Oh him,' said Rhys. 'Got quite a reputation him they say.'

'Can't think why,' said Amelia. 'Seemed very gentlemanly to me.'

'Perhaps it's more the reputation of his father and his uncle I've heard about,' shrugged Rhys. 'Best just to take care though in future.'

'I will, Rhys, don't you worry about me.'

Of course, like most men in that situation Rhys did worry about his niece and after she'd mentioned that Griffith had accompanied her most of the way home from chapel on a couple more Sundays, Rhys tackled his mother about his concerns.

'It's not Amelia's morals that bother me Mam...'

'I should think not,' interrupted Nest. 'You know what the Bible says about the person without sin casting the first stone and that includes our thoughts.'

'I would never think that about my Amelia,' said Rhys, 'but nor is there anything I wouldn't do to avoid our family going through what we did with Caroline.'

Nest paused, silently recalling her first daughter, Amelia's mother. 'I know what you mean Rhys and I share your concerns of course but times have changed and we have to change with them. My own feeling is that we should avoid making any fuss. Amelia is a strong character and knows what's right; she also knows her own mind and how a proper young woman should behave. All we need to be sure of is that she understands that our interest is only in keeping her safe.'

Over the next few weeks Nest made some discreet enquiries about Griffith and his father and uncle. Most people in the village spoke of them as a group of three men, none better than the others. However, those whose judgement Nest regarded as more reliable and who were less given to simple gossip, gave her the impression that Griffith, though sometimes led astray by his father and uncle, was generally well behaved and respectful, especially to girls of his own age. Eventually, when it became clear that Amelia wasn't minded to discourage Griffith, Nest suggested to Rhys and Ceinwen that they pre-empt any problems by suggesting to Amelia that she invite Griffith to visit them at the farm.

One evening during the week before Griffith was due to come, Amelia asked Nest if they could talk privately together.

'Of course *cariad*. Nothing is bothering you is there?'

'Not really Mam, just I don't know exactly what to say to Griffith about our family,' replied Amelia.

'Why do you have to say anything?' asked Nest.

'Well...' she hesitated, 'it's I suppose the difference in ages between me and Rhys.'

'What have you told Griffith already?'

'Nothing at all Mam, I've never said anything to anyone about our family but now with Griffith coming to sit down and talk to us

38

all together I just want to be sure I don't say something I shouldn't.'

'I think it's very simple my dear,' said Nest, taking Amelia's hand gently in hers. 'If your grandfather was here he'd tell you what I have always believed. Telling people the truth, provided you don't hurt anyone else, is always the best thing to do.'

'But I don't want to start gossip about us,' said Amelia.

'Why should you?' asked Nest. 'Unless you have doubts about the sort of man Griffith is. Is he a gossip or a chatterbox?'

'No I don't, but then I also know that he drinks with his father and his uncle and I know how strong drink can loosen men's tongues.'

'Then I think you need to make up your own mind about Griffith,' said Nest. 'If you don't think you can trust him then it's probably best not to tell him anything at all. On the other hand, if you feel your relationship with him might develop into something more serious and if he's the sort of man you want to trust, tell him the truth. That's my advice.'

As if determined to make a good impression Griffith arrived at the Lewis's farm sharp at 3 o'clock the following Sunday afternoon wearing the same suit as he'd worn to chapel in the morning–like most farmers it was his only suit. He'd clearly brushed the dust off his shoes on the back of his trouser legs before knocking on the door.

Over tea and sandwiches Griffith, Amelia and her family chatted amiably. Although the conversation concentrated on farming matters it served to relax all five in the party. After an early meal Rhys excused himself to attend to the animals before nightfall and Ceinwen took the opportunity to accompany him. Almost if at a signal the conversation turned towards Griffith and his family.

'Amelia tells me your family have been at your farm for quite a while, Mr Thomas,' commented Nest.

'Almost 60 years now,' replied Griffith. 'My father's grandfather took on the tenancy first but farming has been in our blood for much longer than that.'

'I was very sad to hear that your mother was only young when she died,' continued Nest. 'It must've been a terrible shock when you were such a young man.'

'Yes, well it's not something I allow myself to think about much,' said Griffith.

'Of course and forgive me for bringing it up,' said Nest. ' I didn't mean to embarrass you Mr Thomas.'

'Oh no, don't worry. Just one of the crosses we have to bear I suppose.'

'I think unexpected death must be the same for most families,' interjected Amelia. 'Even though it's God's will it leaves us with a sadness I don't think we ever forget.'

'I'm sure you're right, Miss Lewis,' said Griffith turning to face Amelia directly, 'though I was unaware that your family had suffered similar sadness. I'm sorry, I didn't mean to be impolite.'

'You're not impolite at all, Mr Thomas,' reassured Nest warmly, looking askance at Amelia as she continued, 'and I'm sure Amelia didn't mean to speak out of turn either.'

'Of course not,' said Amelia hastily, 'I only mentioned it because I thought Mr Thomas might have wondered how it is that Rhys is so much older than me.'

The conversation paused and Amelia found herself looking to Nest, her eyes seeking reassurance and help. Nest tilted her head in question and in response Amelia looked down at her hands folded in her lap. Faced with no alternative and wondering whether Amelia had intended the conversation to turn this way or if it was a simple error, Nest continued as if it was exactly what she was going to say anyway.

'What I think Amelia is referring to Mr Thomas, is that she isn't my daughter as most people believe...'

'I had no idea, Mrs Lewis,' stammered Griffith caught unawares by the change in topic. Nest smiled at him indulgently and continued.

'Please don't be embarrassed,' said Nest, 'it isn't some dark horrible secret, simply that Amelia's mother, my daughter Caroline, died when she was young. She'd been a little foolish and made a mistake but then a lot of girls are foolish when they're young. When Caroline was faced with bringing up Amelia alone, her grandfather and I decided we would care for her ourselves. She's been brought up as our sons' younger sister. That's why she calls me Mam.'

'I see, sorry,' stammered Griffith.

'Well you probably don't really see, Mr Thomas, but no matter,' smiled Nest kindly. 'Small-minded people with lots of time and no manners like nothing more than the situation that we were placed in to gossip about. Anyway, Siôn, my late husband, and I decided to tell everyone a little white lie and pretend that Amelia was a niece of his from mid-Wales whose parents couldn't look after her. It wasn't entirely true but nor was it a million miles from complete honesty.'

'I see,' said Griffith, 'and while we're being honest perhaps you'll allow me to explain and put to rest any stories you've heard around the village about life on our farm.'

'Please don't feel obliged to tell us Griffith, just because we've explained our situation to you,' said Amelia, suddenly nervous about what might be revealed.

'No,' said Griffith, 'and frankly I'm pleased to be able to talk to you about it because,' he paused and turned to Nest, 'I am very serious about Amelia and don't want there to be any misunderstandings.'

'I'm sure there won't be,' said Nest, smiling kindly.

'You're kind to say so,' said Griffith, 'but I know some of the things that people say. Both my father and uncle are grown men. Neither of them has a wife and it's not my place to criticise.'

'Of course not, we understand,' assured Nest.

'But equally I don't want you to think that I live the same sort of life as they do sometimes,' said Griffith quickly, anxious to get the fact off his chest.

'It's very grown-up of you to say that,' said Nest, 'and I know Amelia and I appreciate it.' Griffith looked pleadingly towards

Amelia who smiled warmly as Nest continued. 'Now I have some things to do in the kitchen so if you'll excuse me I'm sure you two have lots to talk about.'

Had the villagers been less bigoted and more observant over the next six months they'd have noticed the extent to which Griffith's whole life changed once Amelia came into it. Gaudily-painted women continued to stay at the farm some weekends but now they arrived in pairs not threes. Griffith's attendance at choir practice was punctual and invariably regular, only at seasons when all the farmers were busy working until well after dark did he send his apologies for missing rehearsals. Throughout the long summer Griffith played the part of devoted suitor to the letter, so that it was not a big surprise when, shortly before Christmas, he stopped Rhys when they bumped into each other at the seed merchants in Carmarthen. After a brief conversation they continued on their separate ways. Two days later a postcard addressed to Nest arrived from Griffith asking if he could call on her after chapel on the following Sunday on 'important business'.

'Do you think I should ask him to stay for lunch?' asked Nest when she, Ceinwen and Amelia were washing up after their evening meal. Both of the older women turned towards Amelia even though the question had been asked generally.

'Why're you looking at me?' asked Amelia, partly confused, partly embarrassed.

'I thought perhaps you'd know what important business he wanted to discuss with me,' said Nest glancing at Ceinwen, who smiled and could barely contain herself. Nest turned back to Amelia. 'Are you sure it's really me he wants to talk to Amelia?'

'Mam you're embarrassing Ceinwen,' smiled Amelia avoiding her gaze by looking intently at the floor lest she gave herself away.

'Nonsense,' said Ceinwen. 'Your grandmother could never embarrass me.'

'Oh Mam this is intolerable,' said Amelia. 'We'll just have to wait until Sunday and see what he says then,' she said gathering up her sewing and hurrying from the room.

Nest and Ceinwen managed to suppress their giggles until they heard Amelia close the parlour door behind her, stifling their amusement behind cupped hands.

'You're very naughty Mam,' said Ceinwen.

'I assume you know what he's planning to ask me?' said Nest.

'Yes, well I guessed, because he saw Rhys the other day when they met at the seed merchant. He asked Rhys if he should talk to him or you about Amelia and of course Rhys told him that you were her grandmother and he was only her uncle so he should talk to you.'

'Sensible man that husband of yours Ceinwen. He'll go far,' said Nest.

The following Sunday when Griffith and Amelia arrived at the farm together after morning worship, Rhys was finishing up in the barn and Nest and Ceinwen were taking advantage of some unseasonable sunshine and shucking peas together seated at a trestle table outside the kitchen window. Together they couldn't resist having a little more fun at Griffith's expense.

'I expect you know why I've asked to speak to you Mrs Lewis?' asked Griffith.

'No idea at all Mr Thomas but it must be serious because you called me Mrs Lewis. Are you going to make me a generous offer for the farm that I could consider?'

'Oh no, Mrs Lewis,' started Griffith.

'A less than generous offer then perhaps?'

'Oh no it's not about the farm at all, Mrs Lewis,' he stammered as Rhys joined the two women.

'Then Mr Thomas you intrigue me, what can be so important that you want to ask?' smiled Nest.

'I want to ask Amelia to marry me,' blurted out Griffith.

'Just that?'

'Well, yes,' said Griffith, reddening very quickly.

'Should we be talking about dowries do you think?' teased Nest. Rhys smiled at Ceinwen.

'Well, I don't know,' said Griffith, suddenly flummoxed, 'should we?'

'Probably not,' said Nest in a more relaxed tone, 'because in truth all we have in the world is what you see round us and even if Amelia and I wanted to we couldn't give you that as a dowry.'

'Of course,' said Griffith. 'Can I ask her then?'

'Are you telling me that you haven't already discussed the subject with Amelia at all?' Nest was still enjoying herself.

'Well, only in the very most general sense Mrs Lewis, and definitely not precisely.'

'Then Perhaps *im*precisely,' she repeated thoughtfully before pausing while Griffith began to shake almost perceptibly. 'Well that's good to know Mr Thomas, I'm pleased to hear it and yes,' she leaned forward and squeezed his arm, 'yes, and I'm not teasing you now, you may ask her.'

'Thank you Mrs Lewis, I am so grateful, thank you, really.'

'Mr Thomas, all I have given you is my permission to ask Amelia. I have no idea how she's going to answer, so before you thank me I think you should wait until you hear what she says. She's in the parlour.'

'I will, Mrs Lewis, I certainly will,' said Griffith, hurrying into the farmhouse. Outside the open window Nest winked at Rhys and smiled kindly at Ceinwen before going inside into the kitchen. Soon after, Rhys and Ceinwen joined her.

'Mam you're a terrible tease,' chided Rhys quietly, 'and Amelia is going to be so angry. I doubt she'll ever see the funny side of it.'

'She'll understand,' said Nest with conviction as she plumped up the cushions. 'Why don't you two help me lay the table.' Suddenly they heard a little squeal of delight from the parlour followed by Amelia's voice saying,'Yes, yes, of course I will, yes.' Then the door opened and Amelia burst in followed by Griffith. She threw herself into Nest's arms.

'Griffith's asked me to marry him Mam, I'm going to be Mrs Thomas.'

'Then I hope you'll be as happy as your Dada and I were,' said Nest hugging her granddaughter as a lifetime of memories flooded into her mind.

The wedding was arranged for early in the spring of 1867 during the lull after ploughing. Griffith had been attentive and courteous, bringing small posies of wildflowers to Amelia and Nest, endearing himself to the women and confirming that he'd abandoned the reputation his father and uncle had earned for riotous living.

Shortly before the wedding a local landowner got in touch with Griffith. He'd heard he was looking for a farm to rent on his own account and asked if he'd be interested in a 92-acre holding known as Troedyrhiw Farm in Abernant, for himself and his new bride after they were married.

'It's not ideal land,' the agent cautioned, 'mainly near the river and a bit wet but it's not expensive and would be suitable for livestock.'

Griffith and Amelia drove in the trap to Abernant to inspect the farm and agreed that although the land near the river was, as the owner had said, rather damp, it would be satisfactory for a start and the annual rent was within the limits of what they could afford. The farmhouse was old and needed some repairs but, with the enthusiasm of young lovers for their first home, Griffith and Amelia took on the tenancy for an initial three years. The rest of the family remained at the farm in Newchurch but sadly, before the first year was out Nest fell ill with tuberculosis, then a common and fatal disease, and within six weeks she had passed away. At around the same time, Griffith and Amelia had found out how expensive the repairs needed at Troedyrhiw Farm were going to be, so to make a steady income Amelia took a teaching position at the little school in Abernant, starting in the autumn term.

By the time the renewal of the farm tenancy became due Griffith and Amelia had rectified most of the faults in the farmhouse so that the building was now warm and dry. Unfortunately, rectifying the problems with the land was more of a challenge and the farm–that in English meant "at the foot of the hill"–had truly lived up to its name and the worst of their expectations. As a gesture the landowner renewed their tenancy at the same rate as the previous three years and promised he'd keep them in mind for a better property when one became available.

In the early years of their tenancy at Troedyrhiw Amelia suffered three miscarriages and without Nest around to reassure her she began to worry that she might never have a baby. Then, in early 1873 Amelia fell pregnant once again and this time carried the child to full term, so that shortly before Christmas that year their first daughter was born. The young couple discussed names with the pastor of the chapel in Abernant, explaining that they hoped to be able to choose a more unusual one for their daughter.

'The old Testament is full of beautiful names,' he told them.
'What sort of names did you have in mind pastor?'
'Names like Sarah, Rebecca, Hagar or Keturah.'
'I like Keturah,' said Amelia
'I do too,' agreed Griffith, 'though it sounds a bit foreign.'
'Actually these days many of our parents are choosing names for their children from the Old Testament,' said the pastor, 'and if you prefer you could always call her Keturia or Catriona'
'No I like Keturah, it's unusual but I like it,' said Amelia, and so their first child was baptised Keturah in the traditional way.

Ironically, at about this time Rhys and Ceinwen were also trying to start a family but without success. They'd hoped that they might eventually have a child to whom they could pass on the farm but as it looked less and less likely they decided that they should look out for a smaller property, one that they could manage themselves. By chance, Morgan Edwards, the representative of a large agricultural equipment company who visited them from time to time, chanced to mention a farm in Tregaron, to the north west near the coast, a property that he'd heard might come up for sale later in the year.

'It's a huge property–been owned by the same family for generations,' he said.

'Sounds interesting but we're certainly not looking for a large place,' said Ceinwen, 'more of a retirement farm.'

'Well that's just it. Under the terms of a will this place is to be broken up into smaller farms so that the various sons and cousins can each have part.'

'I don't see how that could help us,' said Rhys.

'The problem is that not all the various beneficiaries want small farms, at least not the size that might suit you. A couple of the brothers in one branch of the family are planning to sell what they've been left–they think of them as almost smallholdings–and emigrate to Australia.'

'Surely there's enough sheep farming opportunities for them in that part of Wales?' asked Ceinwen.

'Perhaps, but the potential for sheep farming in Australia is vast. Both the brothers are married with families of their own and Australia's space suits them best.'

'So what are they waiting for?' asked Rhys.

'Sale of their property in Tregaron, shipping dates, paperwork, all the business of emigration,' the agent went on. 'It's a long time since you could be sent to Australia as a punishment for stealing a sheep; nowadays the Australians are a bit more selective about who they allow to live there!' said Morgan Edwards smiling.

A couple of months later and after a weekend visit to Tregaron, Rhys and Ceinwen agreed to the modest price the brothers were asking for the farm. There was a healthy interest in the Newchurch farm and before the autumn came they'd packed their belongings, bade farewell to Amelia and Griffith, and left Carmarthenshire for the last time. Some of their best furniture that Griffith and Amelia had long admired but that was too large for their Tregaron home they delivered to Troedyrhiw–a gift much appreciated by Rhys' niece and her husband.

Over the next few years Troedyrhiw echoed more and more to the sound of children's voices. Three years after Keturah's birth Elizabeth was born–though she was known as Rebecca which was the closest Keturah as an infant could get to saying her name–and finally two sons; David in 1882, and–six years later, almost as an afterthought–James. In between these children three other infants were born, all of whom succumbed to the childhood diseases that were prevalent at the time.

Unfortunately, over the years Griffith's behaviour reverted to that of his father and uncle in ways that Amelia had thought he'd overcome. He began to drink and did more singing in the pubs than in the chapel choir. Until he put on weight and lost the good looks that had made him attractive to her, he also earned a reputation as a womaniser. Worse, though it was not uncommon at the time, he would also strike his wife and family, especially when he'd had too much to drink. Although such behaviour was accepted as an inevitable if undesirable part of family life and generally went unpunished, the result of Griffith's behaviour was that inadequate work was done on the farm. The health of his sheep and other livestock declined and the condition of the land deteriorated. Although Griffith continued to press the landlord for a new, better property, his neglect of his present tenancy left the agent disinclined to consider his request. Only shortly before the birth of James, his younger son, did Griffith manage to secure a tenancy on a better farm, a smallholding known as Ffoeshelig on a hilltop near Newchurch. Although the land was better quality and the herd of cows they kept could be enlarged, the distance from Abernant meant that Keturah had to resign her position as a schoolteacher there and rely on her dressmaking skills to help the family budget.

In earlier days such skills would have been widely sought but in the previous 20 years large-scale enterprises, like Cambrian Mills in Powys, had successfully developed mail order businesses and were fast becoming the principal manufacturers and sellers of flannel goods. On the other hand, expansion of the dairy herd would later mean that Rebecca had a full-time job delivering milk throughout the district.

At the same time the economy of South Wales was changing rapidly and affecting swathes of the population. Small farms were becoming increasingly unprofitable while the coal mining and iron and steel industries of Glamorgan offered higher wages and more secure employment. So it was that in late 1888 Griffith and Amelia made a decision that would affect their family's future.

After their supper one evening Griffith folded the local newspaper he'd been reading, put his spectacles on the table in front of him and, with a weary sigh, turned to his wife.

'The problem is, *cariad,* we just don't have enough land here to make a better living.' There was a long pause while Amelia decided whether to pursue the conversation honestly and risk her husband starting an argument she was desperate to avoid.

'Look Griffith, I don't want to argue with you; you're the head of the family and make the decisions but you know as well as I do that our problems are not just the amount of land we have,' replied his wife frostily as she put on her apron and began to wash the dishes.

'What do you mean, woman? Are you saying I'm a bad farmer, that I don't know my business?'

'I'm not questioning your ability as a farmer Griffith but I do question the effort and concentration you give to it.'

'I suppose this is all because I don't sing in the chapel choir as often as I used to; suddenly I'm a bad farmer.'

'You find plenty of time to sing in the public house and put more than enough effort into the loose women who gather there.'

'You deny me an occasional mug of beer? Am I to be denied

even a few pleasures in life?'

'I deny you nothing Griffith; I'm just your wife and the children are just your family. I just don't want you thinking that our financial situation is solely to do with the farm. The state of the farm is no-one's responsibility except your own.'

'*Ach-y-fi*. The responsibility ultimately lies with our landlord. He's never been willing to rent us a better property.'

'And he won't do that because you don't put enough effort into the land you've got already. It was just the same in Abernant.'

'You want me to work every hour God gave and not see my *babans* growing up? Bringing up children isn't just a woman's job. They need a father too. I can't do my part if I'm working like a slave.'

'As I said, Griffith,' repeated Amelia calmly, 'I'm not going to have another row but be honest with yourself. All the hours you spent in the pub and with the other women were the hours your children needed you, and before they arrived, hours the farm needed you.'

'Well it's too late to go back now.'

'That it is, Griffith.'

'Then I don't know what the solution is.'

'Well you'd better start thinking of a solution quite quickly Griffith. When they're grown up David and James will need jobs and since all they'll learn here is farming you'd better do something about getting a farm big enough to employ them. Either that or they—or all of us—will have to move.'

'Move? Where to? You know of farms I have not heard of?' said Griffith raising his voice again.

'Not to farms, to the coalfields and the steel mills. There's plenty of firms there crying out for men and paying good wages too. If you can't give the boys jobs in the country then maybe we should move to the Valleys.'

'You want to live in a terraced house always filthy and covered in grime with air that makes you choke and fills your lungs with poison?'

'No, I don't want to live like that but if that's the only place you and our family can earn a living then that's what we might have to do.'

'Well, I'll think on it woman but it wouldn't be my choice, I'll tell you that now.'

'I didn't say it would be my choice Griffith, I just don't think we have any choice at all.'

Conversations like these were repeated over the coming months and in the end Griffith Thomas had to accept that there was no future for him or his family farming in Southwest Wales. Thus it was, that when their son James was still a babe in arms, Griffith Thomas, his wife Amelia, with Keturah, Rebecca, David and the baby, came to Dowlais in Glamorgan. For Griffith, already 40, there was no question of work in the new industries of the South Wales coalfield which was why he chose Dowlais, the closest coalfield village to the Brecon Beacons and the possibility of farm work. He rented a house in White Street, earned regular if unremarkable wages labouring for a tenant farmer just north of Dowlais, and regretted for the rest of his life the hours and days he'd wasted while living in the most beautiful countryside God ever created.

Chapter 4: Keturah, Rebecca, David and James

Amelia flopped down in one of the two padded chairs she and Griffith had managed to bring with them from Ffoeshelig Farm at Newchurch, good chairs that Rhys and Ceinwen had no room for when they moved to Tregaron. Although the farmhouse at Troedyrhiw wasn't large in comparison to other nearby farm properties, housing was very scarce throughout the Valleys and the home they'd managed to rent at 38A White Street in Dowlais was tiny. These were the only comfortable chairs that would fit in the sitting room of their terraced house. The change in life from the calm of the Carmarthenshire countryside to the constant hum of industry in the Valleys was most noticeable to Keturah and Rebecca; for their brothers the noisy and dirty atmosphere of the Valleys was all they'd known. What Amelia observed most quickly was the degradation inherent in the industrial life of Dowlais. There was plenty of work and plenty of money but, she supposed inevitably, work and money brought in their wake people who cared for little else and others who shunned the honest labour that brought the wealth but preferred to take it by temptation or outright theft from those who'd earned it.

Just as Caroline had taught Amelia to read, to recite her prayers and understand the basics of arithmetic, so Amelia made sure even before they went to school that all her children, first the girls but later the boys as well, learnt everything she could teach them, and more importantly, the value of learning itself. Keturah and Rebecca completed all their schooling at Abernant and by the time the family moved to Dowlais Keturah was earning decent wages as a dressmaker and general seamstress considering she was still a girl of 16. Rebecca never shared her sister's nimble fingers nor her patience but from an early age showed a deep and sincere love of animals. Her father's new employer had a small dairy herd on the Brecon Beacons, was happy to take her on and from the outset Rebecca worked in the cowshed, learning to milk and care for the cows and to watch for signs of illness. Once she was old enough to earn adult wages she established herself with a milk round in Dowlais and the adjacent towns.

As he grew Amelia's older son, David like his sister Rebecca, showed a similar disinterest in book-learning. Nevertheless the grounding his mother gave him stood him in good stead when he attended Dowlais Central School. When his statutory schooling was complete, Mr Mathew Hirst, the headmaster presented him with a generous certificate confirming his education. That pleased Amelia who feared the money her son could earn underground in the colliery would turn his young head. Thus she was not a little relieved when Griffith told her that Dewi Evans, a joiner with a house and workshop in Francis Street, a couple of streets away from theirs in Dowlais had offered David an apprenticeship.

'He's got good hands, Mr Thomas,' Dewi told Griffith a couple of months after David had started his apprenticeship.

'Gets them from his Mam, I 'spect. She's good with the needle as well as wi' books.'

'I'll keep me eye on him, but if he goes on like he's started he could make a decent carpenter one o' these days.'

'Least ways it'll keep him out o' pit.'

'Aye, there's a lot to be said for fresh air and a bit of sunlight.'

Just before David started learning his carpentry trade with Dewi Evans, Keturah, his older sister, encountered for the first time Davy Howells, a journeyman stonemason also from Dowlais. They met at the Whitsun fair during her brother David's last year at school. All the nonconformist chapels as well as the various service and social groups had taken tables to sell goods and items of work to raise funds for their organisations. The Moriah Chapel had taken two tables for its ladies to display the assortment of household items they'd made. Not that this young stonemason with a twinkle in his eye and a lightness in his step was looking at the goods on display, for his eye had been taken by the dark-haired, slim girl nervously accepting the compliments from women examining the items she'd sewn during the previous year.

'And you've done all this beautiful stitching yourself?' asked the taller of two elderly women examining an embroidered doily she and her friend were holding between them. The delicate decoration on her dress and matching bonnet suggested she knew from experience what she was talking about and it wasn't empty flattery.

'Well my mam suggested the design and the flowers ...'

'But you did the actual work?' interrupted the shorter, stockier woman.

'Yes, that's mine,' Keturah admitted quietly.

'Well I think it's exquisite, simply beautiful. How much is it my dear?'

'I'll find out.' Uneasy about the business of selling her work, Keturah turned to the pastor's wife who paused in her conversation with another visitor and took over the transaction with an air of natural authority.

'Yes it's beautiful isn't it and entirely handmade. The doily is threepence. And I think you'll find there's a set of matching napkins, six for a shilling,' she said as she searched for the napkins.

'I think the doily will suit thank you,' replied the taller of the two women handing over the silver coin. While the pastor's wife concluded the sale, Keturah became aware of the young man lolling rather than standing against the opposite wall while watching her. Their eyes met and the man smiled confidently. Keturah blushed, averted her eyes and re-arranged the items to cover the space on the table left by the doily that had just been sold. Suddenly a voice interrupted her.

'Have you something you think would please my Mam?'

Keturah looked up and found herself gazing into the laughing, grey eyes that moments before were watching her from the other side of the road and were now opposite her at the table.

'I have no idea what would please your Mam,' said Keturah with some confusion, 'but if you don't see anything you like here, there's two more tables over there.' She pointed towards the other side of the fair.

'Everything in order Keturah?' enquired the pastor's wife appearing at her elbow.

'Thank you Mrs Jenkins, everything's fine.'

'That's good, just call me if you need some help,' and she turned back to her conversation.

'So it's "Keturah" then?' said the young man. 'I'm David, though everyone calls me Davy.'

Keturah, embarrassed by the young man's familiarity, still looked resolutely down at the goods on the table before her.

'How do I get to see your eyes? Will I have to buy a handkerchief?'

'If that's what you think your mam will like,' replied Keturah raising her head and looking directly at the young man. She knew instinctively that unless she dealt with him more firmly the pastor's wife would be back and though she knew the man was flirting with her rather improperly, she was quite enjoying the attention. She certainly didn't want the pastor's wife interfering.

'To be honest I have no idea what my mam would like, 'cept probably to have me dada sober more often. Trouble is, he has to drink to encourage the men in the pub to buy more beer.'

'Got a beer house has he then?'

'Licenced public house, if you don't mind. There's a difference.'

'Well I wouldn't know about that.'

'Maybe not but the pastors and the deacons around Dowlais all know it pretty well.' Keturah was about to interject but Davy continued, 'not the front door mind, but there's a well-trodden path from all the chapels around to the back door of our pub. Specially after Sunday worship.'

'I'm sure you're making this up and I'm not impressed. All the deacons at Moriah Chapel are strictly teetotal. Now I need to serve this lady,' said Keturah with some finality. She turned to a woman who'd arrived with a small child in her arms, but Davy wasn't quite through.

'So it's "Moriah" then? Revivalist are you?' asked Davy referring to the Moriah's reputation for evangelical preaching.

'And what would be wrong with that anyway?' asked Keturah.

'Nothing at all, just so I know what to expect. I'll see you around perhaps,' replied Davy cheekily, aware that he'd come close to offending the girl.

Keturah glanced towards Davy, a half smile brushed almost imperceptibly across her lips as she continued to attend to the young mother.

Three weeks passed before Keturah saw Davy again. Indeed she'd almost given up on the possibility that the attractive man with the grey eyes would come back into her life when she thought she'd spotted him sitting near the back of the congregation at the Moriah Chapel for one of the choir's last concerts before it sang at the Welsh Methodist's choral festival in Cardiff, the *Cymanfa Ganu*. After the concert the audience mixed with their family and friends in the choir before making their way home. Amelia and Rebecca had both come to support Keturah leaving Griffith at home to look after his two young boys, David and his new brother, James, born just a few months earlier.

'Did you enjoy it?' Keturah asked her mother and sister excitedly.

'Wonderful *cariad*, simply beautiful,' said Amelia, 'It was so moving I was almost in tears so many times.'

'It's a pity they seem to give all the solos to the sopranos, sis,' whispered Rebecca. 'Some of the soprano singers are terribly reedy, you know who I mean.'

'Shush,' smiled Keturah, 'you never know who's listening.'

'Well I don't care,' laughed her sister quietly. 'Never did understand what everyone sees in that Myfanwy Phillips. Big bosom, tinny voice. Give me a warm, smooth alto any time.'

Amelia shushed both giggling girls and hurried them out of the door and up the street towards their home. White Street lay on the high ground above the old town and Moriah Chapel on Mount Pleasant Street and as the three walked up Victoria Street Keturah noticed Davy turning out of Francis Street ahead of them. He turned towards them, paused to cross the road but returned to their side of the pavement when he saw them. The steepness of Victoria Street and the unevenness of the flags made animated conversation impossible and as Amelia and her daughters approached the young man striding down towards them, Keturah held her eyes resolutely on the pavement in front of her. Suddenly she was aware that the man had stopped and stepped politely back into the road to let the ladies past. As he did so he raised his hat and said properly but clearly, 'Good evening, Miss Keturah.'

At the sound of her name Keturah glanced up but immediately away again as mother and daughters continued up the hill. As they turned the corner into White Street, Amelia turned round to her daughters walking behind her.

'I didn't know you knew that young man, Keturah,' she said part as a statement, part a question, but Keturah understood from the use of her proper name this was no general enquiry.

'I don't know him Mam. I don't even know his name.'

'Well he appeared to know yours,' she said looking askance in gentle disapproval.

'He was looking at the chapel stall at the Whitsun Fair a few weeks back. He heard the pastor's wife use my name.'

'Still a bit forward mind.'

'Well I didn't give him an encouragement.'

'Just be careful Keturah. There's nothing more people round here like better than gossip.'

'I'll be careful Mam,' said Keturah as her younger sister nudged her gently in the ribs and they walked indoors.

'So what's his name then?' demanded Rebecca as soon as the girls were in their bedroom taking off their cloaks and bonnets.

'I've no idea,' replied her sister testily.

57

'Oh yes and I was born in Bethlehem last December,' said Rebecca.

'Hush, girl! Mam'll go mad if she hears you talking like that.'

'Then tell me his name or shall I guess? Give me a clue, what's the first letter?'

'D,' Keturah started, 'oh... alright, it's Davy.'

'Davy, Dai or David? There's plenty around so you need to be sure which one you're talking to,' teased Rebecca.

'I've no idea and that's the truth. All he said was that his name was David and people called him Davy, and that's all.'

'Nice eyes though,' continued Rebecca.

'Didn't notice.'

'Well keep your eyes open next time girl or some other lass'll take him.'

'Then they can have him. He's far too big for his boots.'

A couple of evenings later while Amelia was nursing James through a bad cold, Griffith had gone to the pub and David was busy with the books his mam had given him to read. Rebecca, who was washing the dishes with Keturah said, 'I suppose you know your Davy's dada's got a pub up Dowlais Top.'

'So what? And he's not "my Davy".'

'Just thought you'd like to know.'

'Sounds like you're more interested than me.' Their conversation paused, until Keturah said, 'how did you know anyway?'

'Know what?'

'Stop teasing Rebecca! How did you know his father's got a pub?'

'One of the milkmaids knows him. Sounds like she's set her cap at him.'

'Good luck to her then.'

'Says he's a good kisser.'

'Rebecca! Don't talk like that, Mam'll hear and we'll both be in trouble. Say no more and let that be the end of it.'

'Which you obviously don't want.'

'Mind your own business, I think you and those lasses at the farm have too much time to gossip.'

'It's part of the job. When you work with your hands you can chat with your mouth and ears.'

'Idle gossip that's all it is–and bound to make trouble in the long run.'

'Keturah, seriously, anyone would think you've joined a convent.' Keturah looked genuinely shocked at the suggestion that she might be a Catholic, but her sister continued, 'Boys and girls like spending time together, it's natural. It's not like I'm suggesting you marry him for goodness sake. He's just a boy and a good-looking one too and that's all I'm saying.'

'Plenty of time yet,' said Keturah untying her apron and leaving the room.

As it happened a couple of weeks passed before Keturah laid eyes on Davy again and when she did his right arm was in a sling. She was leaving the greengrocer on Victoria Street with a basket of shopping as he was about to go in. He stepped back to allow her to exit.

'Morning, Miss Keturah,' he said as politely as before. 'I'd offer to carry your basket for you but...' he said pointing to his arm.

'Oh dear,' said Keturah, 'no problem anyway it's not heavy. But your arm, is it broken?'

'Greenstick,' he said.

'They's nasty I believe,' said Keturah screwing up her face in sympathetic disgust. 'How'd it happen?'

'A lintel I was working on slipped and fell on me. Lucky it was only for a small window.'

'Is that what you do, then?' she asked setting down her basket beside her on the pavement.

'Yes, mason, stone mason.'

'At Crossley's, next the Ironworks?'

'That's the firm but I work all over since I 'came a journeyman.'

'That's posh then, "all over",' said Keturah playfully mocking the distinction he was making.

'It's not bad for a boy of my age. Most are still serving their time, apprentices like.'

'Well,' said Keturah, picking up her basket, 'fascinating though the career progression is in stonemasoning, I must get these vegetables home for my mam. I hope your arm heals quickly. Good day journeyman stonemason Davy.' She smiled to soften the sarcasm.

'I could walk you home Miss Keturah,' he offered.

'Well that would hardly do much good to your reputation with the milkmaids and others, walking with a girl and her carrying the shopping. Thank you I'll manage,' and she turned and started up Victoria Street.

'Shall I see you again then?' called Davy.

'Well you know which chapel we worship at,' replied Keturah turning and cocking her head playfully before continuing home.

When another two or three weeks passed during which Keturah saw nothing of Davy, she wondered whether she'd given him enough encouragement or if her determination not to appear forward or improper had backfired. On the fourth week, a rainy, early-autumn Sunday, she was surprised to see him, smartly dressed and behaving politely in the congregation at morning worship at Moriah Chapel. Throughout the service it was all she could not to stare at him and, when the downpour intensified at the end of the service and she made her way to the exit with her mother, her heart surged when she saw him waiting outside with a large, very new-looking umbrella.

'Morning Miss Keturah, Mrs Thomas,' he said raising his black bowler hat. 'May I offer you some shelter as you walk home?' To Keturah's complete surprise her mother replied immediately, 'I have my umbrella thank you Mr Howells, but Keturah would appreciate the shelter I'm sure.'

'Can you believe it?' Keturah asked Rebecca as soon as her sister returned from milking the cows that afternoon.

'What's so surprising? Mam's not blind. She knows a handsome man when she sees one.'

'But she knew his name as well. Called him Mr Howells indeed.'

'So our Mam's not so far behind the door as you thought. Seems she's been asking around too,' smiled Rebecca, almost bursting for Keturah to ask her all the details.

'So you've been gossiping again then have you?'

'You told me off for gossiping not long back, so don't accuse me,' she paused. 'On the other hand I would never dare to tell my mam a lie when she asks me a question.'

'Rebecca! You Jezebel!' hissed Keturah, barely able not to shout.

'So it's Jezebel now is it? I'll be Delilah too before I'm Mary Magdalene herself, and all so you can be the Vir...' as the door burst open and the girl's mother stood staring from one to the other, barely able to speak.

'I will not have this blasphemy in my house at any time and certainly not on the Sabbath! If you two want to be treated as adults you'll have to start behaving as adults and not a pair of squawking fishwives. Now down to the scullery both of you. There's plenty of work there for idle hands.'

By autumn of 1894 Keturah and Davy had 'graduated' from meeting covertly, then spending time together on the hills above Dowlais finally to 'walking out' together openly. Neighbours assumed that it was only a matter of time before their marriage was announced. Griffith and Amelia's early reluctance to approve of the relationship was won over largely by Davy's easy charm and the consistent good reports they heard about his behaviour and work. For her part Keturah was completely besotted. Unfortunately just after Christmas the bubble of happiness in which they were all living was broken by Keturah's realisation that she was pregnant. Davy's first reaction saddened her greatly; that they should go to Cardiff and seek an illegal abortion. Keturah, aware of the circumstances of her mother's birth felt betrayed by Davy's selfish and single-minded proposal and asked him point blank if all the promises and professions of love he'd made and she'd echoed meant anything at all or were they 'just words'. In an instant it dawned on Davy that he was about to lose the girl who'd never ceased to attract him since he'd first met her at the sale of work.

'I'm sorry Keturah. I was being utterly selfish and self-centred. Fact is that like everyone else I'd got used to the idea of getting married to you and starting a family. I don't know what I was thinking. I love you Keturah.'

'And I love you Davy boy, as much as ever. I wanted the same as you. It seems to me all we're doing is getting things in the wrong order.'

'So what do we do now *cariad*?' he asked shyly.

'You put on your suit, a clean shirt and brush your shoes and ask my father if he'll let you ask me to marry you,' said Keturah squeezing his hand.

'But I've already asked you.'

'Then pretend you haven't.'

'Won't he guess?'

'Yes but I expect he'll pretend too.'

In fact that was the easy part. Much more difficult was the matter of where they'd wed. Amelia was absolutely set on a wedding at Moriah Chapel and even Griffith could see how it was probably the right thing to do even though his attendance at chapel was now confined almost solely to Christmas. On the other hand Davy's parents were implacably against any religious service, principally because in all the time they'd been in the business of selling alcohol all the churches had preached against it and thus against their living. In the end Eli Passmore, the pastor at Moriah Chapel devised a solution that, although it pleased no-one completely, was not objected outright by anyone either. Thus a civil wedding at Merthyr

Registry Office was arranged for Friday, 25th October 1895, and the pastor sought God's blessing on the union during morning worship at Moriah Chapel the following Sunday.

Unfortunately Fate intervened again and in early April after sliding and falling on a paving stone made slippery by a sudden rainstorm, Keturah miscarried. Amelia was strict in her determination that this situation would not become public knowledge and Keturah and Davy promised that nothing would be said to anyone else, either in their own family nor among their friends.

Although Amelia was worried that Fate would once again intervene the wedding went off without a hitch–at least if you discount the misspelling of Keturah's name on the certificate. The registrar complained with some determination that it was Keturah's handwriting that had caused him to write her name as Keturia. Happily for the wedding, Keturah's father was absolutely (and rather loudly) forceful in his insistence that the registrar correct the mistake. Since it was clearly a clerical error in the Registry Office, after a minor hiatus the certificate was redrawn and the couple were declared legally man and wife. Following the civil ceremony and a wedding breakfast well-supplied with beer, Davy and Keturah spent the first night as man and wife at Merthyr's Imperial Hotel.

'Bit grand for a stonemason,' reflected Griffith to a fellow farm worker some weeks later.

'Oh come on Griff,' he replied, 'give the boy credit for doing the best for his new wife.'

'If I didn't suspect it was more a matter of his father, a publican remember, doing a deal with someone he knows in the trade, I might be more impressed.'

'Good looking boy mind.'

'Oh aye, he's got the looks alright but he knows it too. My Keturah will have to keep an eye on him mark my words.'

'You sure it's not just an old, wiser man and father speaking.

Griff *bach*?'

'What do mean? I'm only saying what I see.'

'And what were you like at his age? When you were newly wed?' Seem to recall you telling me some rare old stories about life with your Uncle Aron,' said Griffith's workmate winking.

'Well, yes, Uncle Aron, now he was a lad.'

'That's all I'm saying boy.'

'Yes but he was a widower.'

'I dare say but you understand what I'm getting at.'

Davy's mates too kept reminding him what he was missing now he was married, partly in fun for they admired Keturah and partly more seriously for some were not a little jealous of Davy. Like so many married men found once the newly-wed passion had worn off the same opportunities and distractions existed as they had before they were married, and gradually Keturah realised Davy was coming home increasingly later in the day and even when he told her he was going out with his pals, he was staying out later and later.

Davy had long since realised that not only were his good looks and particularly his eyes much appreciated by the girls but that he had an easy gift for talking. Not only that but few girls seemed very bothered by the fact that he was married, indeed more than one whispered when he told them that being married would make him extra careful and encouraged him to take even greater pleasures and risks. Nor, being Davy, could he resist bragging to his pals about his conquests, and the fact that he was a married man behaving as he always had, made some even more admiring.

Throughout this period the growth and maturity of the Non-conformist sects continued with the same fervour and Davy's employers had become well-established in the repair and building of chapels through the South Wales coalfield but especially in the Taff valley. That meant that Davy, already a journeymen stonemason by reason of his hard work and attentiveness during his apprenticeship, was also required to work in other towns nearby. That not only meant he left the house he and Keturah rented in Francis Street at irregular times but that he arrived home at different times at the end of the day as well.

'Got a good few advantages has my job,' Davy bragged to his pals one evening as he lingered over a few glasses of beer with a couple of old friends, Robert and Alun Jones.

'What, better than working down the pit with us?' asked Alun.

'Of course. Think about it. What happens when your shift ends?'

'Cage brings us to the surface and we go home, has us tea and then come down the pub.'

'Yes, but what tells you shift's finished?'

'Factory whistle of course,' said Robert dismissively.

'And who hears the whistle?'

'Oh right,' nodded Alun, 'wives and mothers.'

'Exactly,' said Davy.

'Now I don't have a whistle tell everyone when I'm OK to go home,' winked Davy.

'So your Keturah never knows exactly when you'll be home?'

'Well, she could always ask old man Davies in the accounting office, he keeps my time-sheets, but as long as I'm careful and get home at roughly the time it says on my sheets, I'm OK.'

'So you're saying you're still seeing as many girls as you did before you were married *bach*?'

'I'm not saying anything, but do you see me smiling any less than I did before I was married? Have you heard of a new order of monks?' At this both Robert and Alun laughed loud and long.

'So where you working at the moment Davy, lad?'

'Aberdare. New Zion chapel there.'

'Good long walk over the mountain every day then?' asked Alun.

'No I take the train, saves my energy, *bach*,' smiled Davy, 'some of the ladies I've known can be very demanding if I'm not in tiptop condition.'

'Well you're a braver man than me. I wouldn't take that train if you paid me, an' I work underground, mind.'

"Built by Isambard Kingdom Brunel himself. That not good enough for you?' asked Davy.

'Brunel? Overblown self-publicist if you ask me. Look what happened to his Great Eastern. I for one am not surprised this tunnel's collapsed. Damned silly name he's got too, who else you know called Kingdom?'

'Well if you're getting on to names, this is time for me to go home to my ever-loving wife Keturah,' said Davy draining his glass, 'see you boys later this week.'

In fact, with his pals in the pub and elsewhere Davy was content to convey an attitude of devil-may-care towards girls but truth be told, for probably the first time in his life he was deeply in love. So too was Keturah and she returned his physical affection with at least as much passion as her husband. Thus it came as no surprise to either of them when, five months after they were married Keturah announced to Davy that she was expecting their first child to be born in late autumn 1896. Because she'd miscarried the baby she was carrying before she and Davy were married she was naturally reluctant to announce her pregnancy but by late spring it was obvious to most women anyway. Amelia and Rebecca, Keturah's mother and sister, appointed themselves principal midwives as the time for the birth approached. Needless to say Davy's mother was slightly offended that she'd been rather sidelined by Keturah's family but in reality the part she played in the running of the family pub limited the extent to which she could help. Since this was Keturah's first baby, the birth was, as women often found, rather difficult but, with Amelia's experience as a mother and Rebecca's love for her sister, on Christmas Day 1896, Keturah delivered a healthy baby boy she and Davy named William for his grandfather and Noel for the season.

Compared to the open-air life the family had enjoyed in Carmarthen, conditions throughout the Valleys had none of the healthy atmosphere they'd enjoyed before. Smoke and steam from the factories, sometimes laden with coaldust, mixed with winter fogs that slurped and rolled along the valleys unremittingly for days at a time. Despite this, their baby thrived as did Davy and Keturah's family life and within less than two years a second son was born. Named Griffith Thomas in honour of his maternal grandfather although his birth was straightforward, he was not as healthy as his brother. Ill-health took its toll on his education and a lack of solid learning dogged him all his life.

As if in answer to their parents' prayers, Davy and Keturah's third child, another lively and bright son was born in the middle of 1900. Although he suffered somewhat from the same unhealthy living conditions in the coal mining and steel making valleys as his brothers, Baden, as he was known, showed from an early age an innate intelligence not shared by his brothers.

Unfortunately for the marriage Baden's birth meant that Davy was now sharing the house with three infants under the age of five. The result was that Davy lapsed back into his old ways, drinking and chasing girls. The couple rented a larger house in Tredegar in a valley to the east of Dowlais. Here Keturah needed her husband's support more than ever but the move only served to exacerbate their problems. The result was a general deterioration in family harmony which on occasions erupted into physical violence by Davy against his wife. By the spring of 1901, their differences had reached breaking point and Keturah had moved back to her parents' house in White Street, Dowlais leaving her other infants, William and Griff, with their father. Of course, Davy couldn't cope without his wife and, with profuse apologies and promises to change his attitudes and curb his anger, he persuaded Keturah to return home.

Buoyed by his wife's unchanging commitment to their marriage and their family, Davy's good intentions held firm for the next five years with only a few brief lapses. During this time two girls and a fourth son were born to them. Amelia and Elizabeth were born two and four years respectively after David Baden. Daniel, their last-born child came along a year after his younger sister. Unsurprisingly all the children inherited their parent's Celtic dark, almost black hair and although Noel, Baden and Lila inherited their father's grey eyes, the others all had deep brown eyes. Sadly and perhaps as a harbinger of his ill-health to come in later life Daniel suffered with asthma from his earliest days. Later, during his childhood he also endured annoying bouts of acne, the scratching of which meant he reached adulthood with badly marked facial skin. As well as their 'christened' names all the children had names by which they were known in the family. Inevitably Daniel, named after his father's brother, became Danny. William Noel became Noel, Griffith, like most Welsh boys with that name, was called Griff and David Baden was called Baden to avoid confusion with his father. Amelia, named, naturally, for her grandmother became Millie and the childhood name she called her sister, Lila, also stuck even as they grew.

There might have been more children had the relationship between Davy and Keturah not descended into a maelstrom of accusation and counter-accusation mainly concerning Davy's behaviour and infidelities. Along with that Davy's drinking continued to the point at which Keturah demanded that he leave their house until he was sober. The dichotomy she faced had no simple solution; when Davy was around, disagreements flared into arguments; when he was away for days and later weeks on end, the home was calm and peaceful but Keturah was left to bring up their children alone.

As so often happens, and through no fault of her own, things got even worse for Keturah. During a particularly severe winter shortly before Daniel was born and while Davy was absent on another 'bender', Keturah's parents died. Just as Siôn, Amelia's father had perished in bad weather, so too Griffith, her husband, had fallen badly while trying to rescue a herd of sheep in a snowstorm on the Brecon Beacon hills above Dowlais. Amelia, distraught by the second instance of death due to a caprice of Nature, died, according to her doctor of a broken heart not long after she'd buried her husband. Thus ended an unplanned and unexpected chapter in the family story. Begun in recrimination and tragedy, the outcome laid the foundation for the next generation, a generation that would know grief and sadness but also great happiness as well.

Chapter 5: Noel, Griffith, Baden Millie, Lila and Daniel

Sadly, by the time James was old enough to work, wages down the pit as well as in the iron works had started to fall. Trades unions had set coalfield against ironworks and against other mining areas in England and even in Scotland. With neither national organisation and bargaining, nor a strong central organisation capable of agreeing common grievances the unions wanted to pursue, the mine-owners could choose in which mines or localities they would fight the unions. The influx of men from Ireland, and even the Continent, men who were willing to work for less, further deflated the wages in the pit and less experienced lads like Keturah's brother James had no option but to take what was offered, whether in the colliery or at the ironworks. Safety was still not properly regulated in either industry and in any case was regarded as an expense by the owners, who could be as ruthless as their consciences would allow. In the collieries accidents were still as frequent as they had been a century earlier when the deeper pits were first opened up and when tragedy did strike it often hit an entire village so close was the relationship between industry and community.

It was a constant worry for Keturah, with Noel–her oldest son–working underground at the pit, and his brother Griff an apprentice at the Dowlais Iron and Steel works with his Uncle James. One morning, shortly after the morning shift had started, the Dowlais Ironworks' siren mewled its eerie, sickening cry, and Keturah, in the middle of ironing her family's clothes, felt certain her family's name on its shrill wail. It fell to her husband to be the messenger.

'Keturah *cariad*,' he said quietly as he entered the back door into the scullery. Keturah looked up, intrigued by the gentle solicitude in his voice though wary of what it foretold.

'Is it our Noel?'

'No. Ieuan Morris, the manager at the ironworks, is coming down to see you.'

'Why's that?'

'It's your brother. James.'

Keturah straightened up and became alert, fearing more bad news.

'What's happened? Has he been hurt?'

Davy was about to speak when there was a knock at the front door.

'That'll be Ieuan, I'll let him in,' he said.

As Davy showed the manager into the room Keturah sank into a chair at the table. Dressed in a smart but well-worn black suit, slightly baggy at the elbows and the knees, their visitor had the air of an undertaker struggling in bad times.

'Mrs Howells, I'm from the Ironworks,' he started.

'Yes?'

'I've some bad news I'm afraid.'

'Yes?'

'It's your brother, James. I would have gone to his parents but...'

'They died earlier in the year. What's happened to James?'

'There was a backblast from the new furnace, you see..'

'Yes, I understand there's been an accident Mr Morris, I heard the siren,' said Keturah, angered by the manager's dithering. 'What's happened to my brother?'

'Molten metal from the furnace burst out and fell on to the men and your brother was hit badly and, it happened so quick and he couldn't get out the way...'

'So what you're saying is that James is dead?' asked Keturah plainly.

'I'm afraid so, Mrs Howells. I'm so sorry.'

The silence following Mr Morris' rather garbled description of the accident was deafening. Keturah lowered her head slowly into her hands and whispered a quiet prayer. Davy, a little unsteady on his feet, went to his wife and put his hand on her shoulder.

'My God, is there no end to my misery?' she said to no-one in particular, covering her face with her hands. No-one spoke. Ieuan Morris fiddled with the brim of his bowler hat and Davy gazed at the floor. Eventually Keturah raised her head, wiped her eyes with the handkerchief she kept inside her sleeve, and addressed herself to the Ironworks' manager.

'Thank you for coming to tell me yourself Mr Morris. Where is my brother now?'

'He's still at the nursing station at the works. There's no rush mind...'

'No, my husband will go to the undertaker and arrange for my brother's body to be removed. My sister and my other brother will want to know when the undertaker is ready. His home is... was with them and I expect they'll want him to lie there.'

'Of course, Mrs Howells, and you and your family have my deepest sympathy and that of the owners.'

'Yes I'm sure, thank you,' replied Keturah neutrally.

'I always promised I'd never make coffins,' Keturah's younger brother David said to his family that evening, 'but I'm damned if I'm going to bury my brother in someone else's box.'

'There's kind you are *Dai bach*,' said his sister Keturah affectionately. 'I'll pay you for the timber mind.'

'Don't be daft Sis. Dewi, Mr Evans, has already given me some tidy wood and told me I can do some of the work in normal hours. It's the least I could do. You'll have quite enough to worry about already. I'll take care of his casket,' David reassured his sister. Among the other things she had to do was to make sure her husband was sober and wearing clean clothes.

The funeral procession from the Thomas family home in White Street to Moriah Chapel was led by Keturah, with her husband Davy on one side of her and her sister Rebecca on the other. All wore black, the ladies with hand-embroidered black lace veils over their faces. Keturah's brother David, adored by his nephews and nieces who were all anxious to be next to him, followed immediately behind, also clad in black. As usual in such a close-knit community the chapel was filled to overflowing. The choir sang its heart out and the pastor, Evan Herbert, his bush of prematurely grey curly hair, trembling with emotion, spoke of James's young life ended too soon. It was a situation with which many in South Wales where whole families might be working in dangerous industries, were all too familiar and parents in the congregation surreptitiously moved closer together as they listened. After the service, the Thomas and Howells families and their extended kin followed the hearse, drawn by two impeccably groomed black horses, to the cemetery at Pant where the young lad was laid to rest alongside his father and mother.

Less than two weeks after the funeral Davy's own parents passed away as well. Both contracted severe food poisoning from a joint of beef that his father told his wife he'd won at cards but which was subsequently discovered to have been stolen from a consignment of condemned meat on its way to be destroyed. The licence of their premises was transferred to Davy, and with his family he moved to the Rolling Mill public house at 1 Horse Street.

Even as the last of Amelia's generation still living in Wales was laid to rest and the country was recovering from the Boer War in South Africa, the clouds of an even larger confrontation loomed. Perhaps the only relief in this panoply of misery and misfortune was the fact that Baden, Keturah's third son was achieving good marks and reports from school. Whereas Noel and Griff had left at the usual finishing age of 14, Baden's head teacher, Gareth Jenkins, encouraged his parents to let the boy remain in education.

'Frankly,' Jenkins said when he came to Davy and Keturah's private sitting room at the back of the pub one evening, 'I think he's a gifted lad. He could go far.'

'Well, that's good to hear Mr Jenkins, but look around you, we're working folk of modest means. Do we look as if we could afford to pay for Baden to be given all the learning you say he's capable of?'

'Well first of all Mr Howells, allow me to assure you that I do not make any judgements about people when I'm invited to a pupil's home to discuss his academic progress,' said the schoolmaster, anxious to dispel any notion that he was patronising the boy's parents.

'Well, put it this way,' interrupted Davy. 'I'm sure we both know there are some families in the neighbourhood that are doing well and can even afford to advertise their wealth by having second pianos standing in the rain outside their homes.' The teacher nodded his understanding. 'Well this isn't one of them,' said Davy defensively. Although Keturah's face never gave a hint of what she was thinking, it did occur to her that one of the main reasons they weren't as well off as many others in the town was that Davy spent so much on beer and other women. Fortunately, the schoolmaster continued.

'Of course I understand all that but what I have in mind is entering Baden for a scholarship to Cyfarthfa.'

'To where?' asked Davy puzzled since he only thought of the former iron-master's property as a museum.

'Cyfarthfa Grammar School, starting at the castle this year. As you know entrance to the grammar schools is by competitive exam. I think, with a little help perhaps, Baden could do well.'

'But there are other costs I'm not sure we could afford,' said Keturah.

'The school would pay his tram fares but, yes, of course, parents have to provide the school uniform,' said the teacher.

Keturah, still wearing a concerned frown, continued. 'I'm flattered and pleased of course Mr Jenkins, but are you sure Baden really has a chance? None of our other children has shown any leanings towards academic ability and I wouldn't want Baden to simply be making up the numbers for the exam. What I'm saying is that while I think we could probably manage the cost of his uniform at a pinch, and I realise no-one can give guarantees of success, I don't want to give Baden any false hopes.'

'Well, of course, as you say Mrs Howells, the exam is competitive and none of us can guarantee how Baden will manage on the day but I assure you he has the ability. If you agree I will give him as much time and help in preparation as I can. But, the final decision is for you and your husband,' he said turning to Keturah and Davy in turn.

Once Millie and Lila, Baden's younger sisters, and their baby brother Daniel, had got over their giggles at the idea of their brother taking a 'special exam', the whole family swung behind him in support. Even Davy managed to spend more time with his son and less behind the bar and when the Saturday of the exam arrived Baden's mother and father both accompanied him on the tram to Merthyr.

After the exam Baden was quiet and subdued.
'Well come on boy, tell us all about it,' demanded his father.
'I don't really know, Dada. There were four sections...'
'Four, by Jove!'
'Davy! Language please,' said Keturah firmly.
'Sorry *cariad*. Four eh? And what subjects?'
'Mathematics, History, Composition and Geography.'
'My, I didn't know you knew anything about history or geography,' said his father.
'That was what Mr Jenkins was teaching him when he came round in the evenings–the evenings you were busy in the bar Davy,' scolded Keturah.
'Well, I'm impressed, boy,' continued Davy ignoring his wife's criticism. 'When do you hear, get the results, you know?'
'They write in about two weeks,' explained Baden.
'So now we hope for an early letter,' said Davy with pride and, thought Keturah, a little too much presumption.

When the letter did arrive exactly two weeks later Keturah mentally apologised for doubting her son for, as Mr Jenkins had predicted was possible, Baden was awarded a place at Cyfarthfa Grammar School. It also earned him a mention by name in the paper of which Davy bought half a dozen copies to show his customers at the pub.

The following spring arrived so late in the South Wales valleys that some wondered if it would come at all. By the time it did, life at the Rolling Mill had become even worse for Keturah than it was before Davy had inherited it. Probably the worst legacy to bequeath a drunk is a pub and that proved right in Davy's case. The only tiny benefit for Keturah and the rest of her family was that at least she had an income, albeit one that took all her time and the help of her children to maintain.

Of course Davy, like all drunks, justified his excessive drinking. His excuse was the old saw that it encouraged his patrons to buy more drinks themselves. No-one liked a landlord who didn't drink while they spent money buying round after round, he claimed. And only a drunk can see the logic rather than the futility of that argument.

Then he started sleeping longer in the mornings, leaving the ordering, the cleaning and the business of the pub to Keturah, after she'd got the children washed and fed and off to school or, in the case of the two older boys, off to work. And soon she left him in bed, sleeping off the previous night's drinking. If she woke him any earlier there'd invariably be an argument if not a fight, and frankly it was easier to avoid the problem and get on with the work herself.

Sundays were the worst. Pubs were legally closed but every pub in South Wales had a back door and a well-trodden path from the chapel or the church that led men of every persuasion and none from God straight back to drink even on the day of rest. Keturah's greatest pleasure, apart from her children, had been singing in the choir at Moriah chapel in Mount Pleasant Street but such pleasures became a thing of the past once her husband took to sleeping off the effects of the previous night's drinking and men, god-fearing and otherwise, wanted to slake their thirsts.

As the years passed things got worse, not better as Davy took to staying away for nights at a time. If Keturah hadn't known that he'd be sleeping off the excesses of his drinking she might have thought he was being unfaithful, but in the state he'd drink himself into she knew that no matter how much he was tempted he'd be physically unable. That didn't make her shame any easier to bear on the streets of Dowlais but at least she could look those women who made a living from their beds straight in the eye. Ironically it wasn't another woman who gave Dowlais its biggest laugh at her expense but a horse.

Just before Easter, Davy disappeared and was gone from the pub for longer than ever before. As usual, the oldest boys scrubbed floors and washed pots from daybreak till night to help the family get through the religious festival. Then, on the Saturday after Easter, Davy turned up, leading a horse. And not just any horse but a fine-looking–though ungroomed–stallion that towered above Davy.

'Won him from an Irishman playing cards. Beautiful animal. Did you ever see anything like him?'

'And that makes it all OK? What are you going to do with it?' asked Keturah.

'Not do with "it" *cariad*. I'm going to ride "him" to victory!'

'And when did you learn to ride a horse?'

'I'll learn.'

'Well the first thing you need to learn is how to get on its back. You'll need a stepladder.'

'That's not difficult, the Irish showed me.'

'And how drunk were you both when this lesson took place?'

'I was as sober as a judge. Mind, the Irish was a few sheets gone but he'd just lost his fine horse.'

'Well, where are you planning to keep this poor creature now it's here? This is a pub not a stables.'

'Like I said he's a "him", not an "it", *fy caru*, and I'll tether him in the field just beyond Dowlais Top.'

'From where the next passing tinker can steal him back. Well the sooner that happens the better, Davy. Now, get your horse out of the yard and come and help me clear up. It's been a busy evening.'

'Aw *cariad*, I'm bushed. I've been leading him all day. Get Noel to help you this time.'

'Maybe you should have got the Irishman to teach you to ride and you wouldn't have had to walk. Noel *and* Griff have been helping me every day and night these past weeks while you've been gone winning horses at cards. They're bushed too.'

'Then they'll know what to do by now won't they? I'll take my horse up to the field and we'll talk in the morning.'
With that Davy led his horse past the crowd that had gathered.

'Show's over everybody,' Keturah called to the onlookers and they began to mumble their way out into the street.

She didn't hear Davy get up the next morning, though later she gathered it was before five. Noel and Griff didn't stir either when he crept into the boys' room and woke Baden. Motioning him with his finger to be quiet, Davy led the boy downstairs. In the kitchen he whispered to Baden to get his britches on and wrap a faded woollen scarf round his neck against the morning cold.

'We'll take the horse for a ride, son,'

'But I can't ride, Dada.'

'The Irish can ride soon as they're born, so it can't be too difficult for a bright young Welshman.'

Father and son made their way out of the yard and up Horse Street, where all the windows were tightly closed against the cool spring morning. Passing the station they walked up the street rising towards the foothills of the Brecon Beacons.

'He's awful big, Dada,' said Baden as they approached the horse.

'I'll help you up. It's a great view from up there. And you'll look right grand too.'

'Shouldn't we give him some water? Won't he be thirsty?'

'You can ride him down to the stream. Now, let me fasten the saddle like the Irish showed me and then I'll get you up.'

78

Davy pulled the girth tighter and settled the saddle that had slipped around the side of the horse during the night into its correct position on its back. As he untied its tether, the horse, now free, threw its head back and snorted loudly. Davy spoke gently to the horse in quiet, calm tones.

'Whoa there boy. Gently does it. Let's walk around a bit like the Irish showed me.'

Davy led the horse by the reins and walked him in a wide circle though the horse shied away and pulled on the reins.

'You'll have to be firm with him Baden. He needs to know who's boss. He's got a great spirit but you'll have to curb his enthusiasm. Remember he was bred to run, when you tell him to.'

'I don't think this is a good idea, Dada. Why don't you get Jones the Milk show me how to do it? He's got horses, he could show me.'

'This isn't no milk cart horse, Baden. This'n racehorse, a thoroughbred. Just get on. Riding'll come natural to a bright lad like you.'

With that he lifted his son into the saddle. The horse, sore from not having the saddle off him for days, nor the bit removed from his mouth, thumped his feet on the ground.

'Whoa, there. Hold his head steady with the reins, Baden. Not too tight or you'll hurt his mouth with the bit. That's right. Whoa boy. I'll shorten the stirrups so you can get your feet in them.'

He adjusted the length of the leather strap so his son's left foot sat comfortably in the stirrup with his leg bent in the position taken by race jockeys. That was when he made his mistake. Instead of walking round to the other side in front of the horse as the Irishman had shown him explaining that the horse would stay calm as long as it could see him, Davy walked around behind its rear. Startled, the horse kicked out catching Davy on his left side and knocking him to the ground with a loud snort. That in turn startled Baden perched on

79

the horse's back with just one foot securely in a stirrup. His reaction was to try and balance and in so doing he kicked back with his loose leg and relaxed his grasp on the reins. The horse, sat back on its haunches and with a toss of its head and fire in its eyes, galloped towards the middle of the field. Baden pulled back on the reins but instead of slowing the animal the pain of the bit in its mouth urged the horse to stretch its legs, increasing speed across the grass and down the meadow towards the stream.

Davy, still struggling to his feet, had lost sight of the horse with his son, lopsidedly trying to stay on the horse's back. He yelled out in sheer panic.

'Baden! Baden! Get your foot out of the stirrup.'

Even as he shouted he knew that the boy's natural reaction would be to dig his foot more firmly than ever into the only part of the saddle that seemed to give him any support or stability. Davy knew instinctively that if Baden fell when his foot was still in the stirrup, the horse would drag the boy along as it raced, banging his son like a rag doll along the ground. The thought of the possible results chilled his blood and he raced towards the lower field.

Fortunately Baden hadn't fallen from his mount but leant forward and grasped the horse around its neck, letting go of the reins as he did. The horse, aware that it had a complete novice and not a skilled rider on board, galloped towards the bottom edge of the field and the cool stream. Even the wooden fence posed no impediment and drawn towards the water, the horse lengthened its stride and prepared to jump the fence. Had Baden been with his father when he'd won the horse he'd have heard the Irishman warn Davy that it was a flat racer, not a jumper, and the horse's innate but pathetic instinct to jump merely left it crashing through the fence. The fence was shattered, the horse's chest and belly were badly injured and Baden was thrown some fifteen feet out of the saddle. The stirrup strap was torn away. Baden's left knee was wrenched painfully to the side and his body smashed against the trunk of the willow on the far side of the stream giving him two nasty fractures to his right arm.

Back at the pub, the doctor set Baden's broken arm and bound his damaged knee.

'It'll be six weeks or so before you can put any weight on that knee young fellow, and you'll not be writing in your schoolbooks until the autumn. I've given your mam some aspirin pills that'll take away some of the pain but I'd rather you only took them when the pain was too bad to bear. They're not cheap either and too many could hurt you, so be sensible.'

Keturah paid the doctor and thanked him for coming so quickly.

'Can I offer you a glass before you go, doctor?'

'No thanks Mrs Howells, though it's kind of you considering it's a Sunday,' he winked knowingly. 'I'll drop in at the end of the week to see how young Baden's going. Just keep him warm and let him rest. And no school of course.'

'He was due to leave this summer anyway.'

'Then I guess he's had all the school learning he's going to get. Good day.'

The doctor raised his hat politely and closed the door behind him.

Despite the months it took for him to recover from his accident, Baden remained inspired by the knowledge of the world outside Dowlais and South Wales that Mr Jenkins had drilled into him in preparation for the Cyfarthfa Grammar School exam. Perhaps partly for this reason he was entirely unenthusiastic about the prospect of working in the family pub for the rest of his life. He sought out his former teacher for advice.

'To be honest Baden,' Mr Jenkins began, 'it is a great pity you weren't able to make more use of the opportunity you had at Cyfarthfa. I can't think of a profession–and that's what I think you should aspire to–that wouldn't need a higher level of educational achievement. I know it's an odd, even foolhardy question to ask a boy of 15 but how brave *are* you?'

'Very,' replied Baden.

'Yes, well I said it was a foolhardy question,' continued the teacher smiling wryly. 'What I mean is there's this terrible war going on...'

'I don't think my mother would let me join the army,' interrupted Baden.

'No, well you're too young anyway, but that wasn't what I was thinking. No, my wife's brother-in-law is a director of a small shipping company, sailing out of Barry Docks. They have a regular trade with South America, especially with Argentina–you remember I taught you about the migration of the Welsh to Argentina during the last century?'

'Because they were concerned their culture, language and religion would be forbidden by the English?'

'That's right, good boy. Anyway, if your parents agree I might be able to find you a place on one of their ships.'

'That would be wonderful Mr Jenkins. I'd love that!'

'Before you get too excited remember that German submarines are just as happy to torpedo a merchant ship as a battleship so there's a serious risk of you getting killed.'

'I understand that sir but men get killed down the pits too.'

'That's true but have a word with your parents before you make a decision. Let me know what you decide and I'll find out what the prospects are.'

The decision to allow Baden to sign on as a cabin boy working in the galley of the Daffodil was made by Keturah alone, Davy having been told to leave their home after blackening her eye in a drunken spat. When Mr Jenkins had said the company 'sailed' from Barry he was being precise, for the Daffodil was an old, three-masted barque. Initially the ship had to work hard to make headway across the Bay of Biscay, tacking because of the predominantly westerly winds. As a result Baden was constantly seasick, which didn't endear him to the cook in whose galley he'd been hired to work. Once the Daffodil passed Gibraltar and picked up the north east trade winds, however, progress was faster and smoother and Baden discovered his sea legs and was able to work his full watches. Gradually, as the ship approached the equator, the seas moderated even more and the ship was frequently becalmed until a passing breeze would ruffle the sails and she could resume her journey.

South of the equator the trade winds blew predominantly from the south east, off the ship's port beam. Progress was steady although the lean of the ship into wind occasionally made cooking meals for the crew as they came off watch very demanding. However, it was all part of his new learning experience and by the time the ship docked at Rawson in Chabut province of Argentina where the Welsh colony was concentrated, Baden felt entirely comfortable with the seafaring life. He'd learnt to cook, in fair weather and foul, he'd learnt basic seamanship and how to get along in cramped conditions with crewmen of many nationalities. Most importantly he'd become an independent young man who not only knew his strengths but also when to let modesty prevail–to get along with people.

The return voyage to Wales was relatively uneventful apart from a tropical storm that blew up while they were off the coast of northern Brazil. As the Daffodil neared Wales and Baden found he coped with the storms of the Bay of Biscay, the cook asked him if he intended to sign on for another voyage.

'Mind, it won't be under sail,' the cook said wistfully.

'Why not?' Baden asked.

'The owners have decided the old Daff has done enough.'

'She's sound isn't she? And the wind's free,' said Baden brightly.

'That's true enough, but shippers these days want speed, mechanical winches, regular schedules, even radios soon I daresay if this war goes on much longer–all things old ladies like the Daff can't give them.'

'Are you staying on?' he asked the cook.

'Me? Probably. It'll take a while to get used to an iron tub and a throbbing engine but the sea gets in your blood.'

'Well I think mine's got quite salty so look out for me.'

'So I will, boy, so I will.'

In the event Baden nearly didn't go back to sea at all. When he arrived home his father was absent on yet another of his benders but this time he had left Keturah with broken ribs as well as a bruised face. By the time she was sufficiently recovered Baden had missed several sailings of his employer's ships. Nonetheless, his mother realised her son had formed an affinity with the sea and when she was able to manage the pub with the help of just her other children, she urged Baden to get in touch with the shipping company.

'Look *Baden bach*. Millie, Lila and Danny too are old enough to work now. That means Noel and Griff can do more in the works and at the pit so we'll be fine, I promise.'

'And what about Dada? What if he turns up again?' Baden asked his mother, realising he was speaking of his father as if he wasn't part of the family anymore.

'Noel'll take care of me, don't you worry. Anyway I hear that Dada's gone up to London so I doubt we'll be hearing much from him anyway.'

'If you're sure then, Mam. You're everything to me you know,' said Baden clasping his mother's tiny hand in his.

'I know Baden, I know,' she replied kissing his forehead.

Baden's new ship was a modern steam-driven general cargo ship. As well as two big steam engines that propelled the ship, all the gear for moving and stowing the cargo was driven by steam too. The crew was larger and, with the recommendation the cook on the Daffodil gave the company, Baden was hired as cook with two galley boys to assist him. Although it was already 14 years old, compared to the Daff (as she was affectionately known within the company), the Alwyn Jones, named for the owner's oldest son, was like a different world.

For one thing the galley was modern and getting meals ready for the crew under most sea conditions wasn't the challenge it had been on the Daffodil. Of course the prevailing winds still blew from the same directions but apart from storms and heavy seas, which impeded even the steamship, progress could be made almost regardless of the weather.

Since she could maintain reliable schedules, the Alwyn Jones picked up and landed cargos at many more ports along the coast of South America. From the sugar and spice islands of the Caribbean to the myriad trading ports along the more than 1500 miles of Brazil's Atlantic coast that stretched from the equator to 20° of latitude south, Baden absorbed the sights and sounds, the smells and the tastes of the different cultures as the ship made its way south. In quiet moments off duty when he could smoke a cigarette in a sheltered corner of the deck he mused on the hopes that Gareth Jenkins had inspired in him when he urged him not to waste his talent in the labourious drudgery of manual jobs in South Wales but to explore the world and see what the whole globe and not just what his beloved Valleys could offer.

85

Ironically, a chance for a radical change in his life's direction appeared when the Alwyn Jones made an unplanned call at Montevideo, the capital and main port of Uruguay. The masters of ships like the Alwyn Jones could trade on their own initiative and pick up valuable cargoes as they were offered along the voyage. On this occasion Captain Simmons had been able to acquire a large consignment of agricultural equipment at Rio de Janeiro, a cargo that had not been ready in time to load on the ship on which it had been booked. Captain Simmons had announced the change to the voyage to the officers and before they sailed from Rio the first mate had been instructed to tell Baden to order enough extra provisions to be ready for the ship in Uruguay. Thus it was that Baden became acquainted with Santos y Martínez, a leading ship's chandler in Montevideo.

As soon as the Alwyn Jones had tied up and Uruguayan customs had cleared her certificates and manifests, the chandler's representative was bounding up the gangplank asking for Baden.

'*Señor Ow-lays*,' he demanded of the duty watch-keeper in his strongly-accented English.

'*No habla* boyo,' the duty guard replied offhandedly.

'*Qué?*'

'*No habla la lingo* boyo,' insisted the lad from Pontypridd making only his second voyage to South America.

'*No, Señor Ow-lays, por favor. La cocina del barco. Madre de Dios. Comiendo*,' the chandler persisted to no avail. The watch-keeper was losing all interest and was about to order the man off the gangplank when a Spanish-speaking stoker appeared from the crew accommodation section. The chandler addressed himself to the seaman.

'*Soy el velero, Santos y Martínez.*'

'Eh Taff,' the seaman called, 'He's the chandler. He wants Baden in the galley.'

'Why didn't he say then? Thanks Pedro,' then turning back to the visitor who was mumbling to himself '*Soy el chandler, el velero.*

86

¿Qué es tan difícil?

'Now wait here boy,' said the watch-keeper indicating with his hand that the visitor should remain where he stood, 'and my pal will fetch him for you as soon as he's finished the job he's doing for the first mate, OK?'

'*Si señor, gracias,*' he said cheerily.

Although the Alwyn Jones remained in Montevideo for just two nights, by the time it sailed Baden had got to know the two owners of the chandlery remarkably well. Of course, for Paco Santos and his much older partner, Juan Martínez, creating friendly relationships with those crew members they believed could direct business their way was all part of the job. But, by the time the ship sailed onwards towards Argentina, Baden had spent several hours with the men, eating excellent *tira de asado,* strips of beef grilled over an open fire, washed down with *clericó,* wine mixed with fruit juice, and *grappamiel,* a potent mix of alcohol and honey. Looking back a few days later as the ship steamed its way across the wide mouth of the River Plate en route to Buenos Aires and later Rawson in Argentina where he'd meet the Patagonian Welsh again, Baden felt he'd made more than a mere business friendship with the two men and had begun to understand their heavily-accented English.

After unloading the cargoes intended for the Welsh community in Chabut province, Captain Simmons' original intention was to sail from Rawson to Buenos Aires and then back northward direct to Rio and home. However Fate intervened again and when they were just a day's steaming north of Montevideo, the chief engineer reported a fault in the electric telegraph that the captain used to communicate with the engine room. The two officers discussed the possibility of sailing on and using a ship's telephone to convey and acknowledge his instructions but on the engineer's advice the captain decided to return to Montevideo for repairs. That serendipity gave Baden time to renew his friendship with the two partners in the chandlery and to get more of a 'feel' for the life and culture of Uruguay. With the

87

partners he explored some of the bars and restaurants and one evening found himself with them in a bar where a new dance craze, the tango, was all the rage. Born in the bordellos and pick-up dance halls of the Argentinian and Uruguayan Atlantic ports, the dance was originally little more than an opportunity for the bar girls to encourage and ensnare their clients although in time it would become fashionable on more respectable dance floors. Towards the end of the evening and emboldened by more *grappamiel* than was wise, Baden was led to the tiny dance floor by a beautiful, sultry girl, perhaps a year or two older than he was. Her scarlet dress, made of a soft, sheer material, had a side slit that allowed her to perform the intricate steps of the dance. Occasionally her long dark hair fell across her face and she smiled as she brushed it away with a subtle flick of her fingers. With his hand on her waist Baden was aware of the pressures of her body against his as they danced, and her perfume enveloping both of them. As expert dancers do she felt weightless to him. Her fingers curled inside his palm, her lips brushing lightly past his cheek as if dictated by the rhythm of the music and their hips aligned precisely. It felt to them as if they were alone and not amid a crowd of other dancers. As the tune ended the girl explained to Baden with smiles and tactile gestures that her name was Alejandra. She could speak very little English and she realised that Baden couldn't understand Spanish. Spellbound, Baden lost any shyness or reserve, overwhelmed by desire. Watching the pair, Juan and Paco, familiar with the guiles of the girls who inhabited the bars and dance halls, smiled to each other and went home, confident that Baden wouldn't need their company for the rest of the evening.

The tango was intended to be a sensuous, close-quarters experience that left both dancers completely aware of the other's sexual needs. As the music ended and the dancers moved slowly off the floor, Alejandra leaned provocatively against Baden, her arm holding his hand against her hip and whispered in his ear. He looked blankly at her. She gestured discreetly with her hand conveying her wish that they should go elsewhere together. That gesture Baden understood at once and after discovering that Paco and Juan had already left, he took Alejandra's hand and she gently led him from the bar. Out on the street, Alejandra hailed a passing taxi, an aged American saloon, and drew Baden in beside her on the back seat. She gave the driver an address and told him to turn the rear-view mirror away then turned back to Baden, kissing him long and passionately on the mouth, the breeze from the open window billowing her long hair around their heads as they embraced. As the taxi left the centre of the city she curled up on his shoulder, his hand cradled lightly by hers in her lap, his senses suffused with her perfume. When the taxi stopped Baden found they were outside a small wooden house, little more than a cabin, on a hill overlooking the city. He paid the taxi and as it accelerated down the hill he turned towards the house. Alejandra had opened the front door, leant back and placed one heel on the frame. She waited for Baden to walk up the two steps to the porch then held out her hand, drew him inside and closed the door behind them.

The heat of the night, the intoxication of alcohol and the shared intimacy and the passionate embraces of the dancing led them inevitably and directly to Alejandra's bed. Only as their mutual desire and nakedness drew them to a conclusion did Baden pause.

'*¿Qué?*' queried Alejandra, thinking she'd done something to dampen what she was sure was their shared desire.

'No... no babies,' whispered Baden in her ear.

'*Ah sí,*' replied Alejandra huskily, '*entiendo. No bebé. No voy a quedar embarazada.*' With that simple and sincere assurance, Baden knelt up, Alejandra wriggled beneath him, spreading her hair, still shiny in the half-light, across the pillow and they gave themselves to the darkness and the passion of the night.

'So Baden, what will you do when you get back to Wales? Have you decided?' asked Juan Martínez when they met at lunchtime two days later.

'I've not really given it much thought, Juan,' replied Baden. 'Mr Gareth Jenkins, my teacher, encouraged me to explore the world outside the Welsh valleys before deciding. It was he who introduced me to the owners of the Alwyn Jones and so far all I've seen of the world are the two voyages down to Argentina, this trip and an earlier one last year on the owners' sailing barque, the Daffodil.'

'*Ah sí*, I remember the Daffodil, good ship,' said Juan.

'Do you think any place you've seen so far has enough to hold you there permanently,' asked Paco, whose English Baden found much easier to understand.

'If I said here would you be surprised?'

'Montevideo?' asked Juan.

'Depends how many Alejandra's he met in other ports,' smiled Paco to his partner.

'To be honest,' said Baden, 'and I'm not just saying this to flatter you as Uruguayans, but Alejandra is a very special person.'

'You know that already? After just two nights?' smiled Paco.

'Perhaps not best to make a decision on Alejandra alone,' said Juan.

'There are many bars and dance halls in Montevideo and even more "Alejandras" my friend,' said Paco in clarification. 'She's very pretty, I'll not deny that, and I'm sure she's very satisfying in bed, but that's her job.'

'But it wasn't like that Paco. I didn't pay her any money,' said Baden determined to explain that he'd not fallen for a common bar girl.

'No of course not,' said Paco calmly, 'but the owner of the bar where we took you pays Alejandra to keep men like you, mariners and travellers especially, drinking and eating in their bar. If money gets tight and especially after her looks have begun to fade, I'm afraid the only life that she'll have left will be making the best of what talent and abilities she's got as best she can, if you know what I mean.'

Baden sat quietly, reflecting on what Paco had just told him.

'Isn't that the same for everyone, everywhere?' asked Baden.

'I mean, I have two sisters who I love very much and in fact one of them is very pretty, but they'll both grow and their looks will fade as everybody's does. It doesn't change them as lovely people.'

'Of course,' said Paco, 'but when it is your looks that have kept you solvent, even relatively wealthy, then, as Juan will tell you, your options reduce very quickly. Everybody has to eat.'

Baden was thoughtful and silent, then Paco spoke again.

'But beautiful girls are only part of the equation and I'm sure you'll find them wherever you are, in Uruguay, Argentina or Wales, and believe me Baden, there are many. What there are not are opportunities for earning a living, a good living if you're prepared to work hard and spend wisely.'

'What Paco is getting round to,' said Juan, 'is that I'm not getting any younger and I want to sell my partnership in our business.'

'What Juan wants–well, both of us need–is a bright, intelligent young man who'll work hard, become as prudent a businessman as we are and be a fair partner in our business. We think that man could be you.'

'And live in Montevideo of course,' added Juan.

'Of course,' said Paco, 'I'm biased but I've lived here all my life, never wanted to live anywhere else. Since the last colonial wars left our country a sovereign nation I'm a proud and loyal Uruguayan. Our country has a flourishing export trade in meat, even better now there are efficient refrigerated ships...'

'And the wine trade could one day rival the meat trade, trust me,' added Juan.

'Goodness, gentlemen, this is a lot for a fellow to think about. I'd never thought about going into business until I was much older.'

'Of course, but whoever we take in must be young for there is Juan's life's experience to learn,' said Paco.

'Let's arrange another meeting for the end of the week. We'll get some business friends together and give you the chance to listen to other people's opinions, not just ours,' proposed Paco. 'Then you can decide. Oh, and one of them is a banker; he'll explain how you can finance the partnership if you decide to accept our offer.'

Before the weekend arrived Baden talked to Captain Simmons about the offer he'd been made, stressing that he wanted to keep it a secret until he'd made up his mind.

'Not going to jump ship, though are you boy?' asked the master.

'No of course not, Captain. I signed a contract and that's my word. And if I broke my promise I'd be letting Mr Jenkins down as well as you and the company. It was he who introduced me to the owners.'

'Good man. I'm pleased to hear that. I'll introduce you to the company's banker in Montevideo tomorrow morning. He's a straight man.'

The banker's view was very frank and much less rosy than that of Paco and Juan. He explained to Baden and the captain how politics were changing in Uruguay, how the country was becoming polarised with the Catholics on one side and the Communists and Socialists on the other. In conclusion he said, 'If I was making the decision you're considering I think I'd wait for 10 or 15 years and see how things look then.'

Captain Simmons listened intently to Baden's reaction to what the banker had told them.

'That struck me as a very fair summary. He's certainly not pulling any punches. On the other hand, the war in Europe looks as though it's coming to a close though that'll certainly lead to another period of instability and doubt, so don't assume staying in Uruguay's necessarily a good option. What I'm sure is that we'll need good marine chandlers for as long as there are ships plying the oceans.'

'Thank you, sir. I appreciate your views,' said Baden. 'In fact I have one other consideration and that's my mother. She runs the family pub, only most of the workload falls on her and my two young sisters.'

'Haven't you got brothers? And what about your father? I assume he's still alive.'

'Oh yes, he's alive but unfortunately he's not in South Wales very much and not often sober when he is. Yes, I've two older brothers but one's down the pit and the other one works in the ironworks but he's got a bad chest and isn't well. As well as my sisters I've got a younger brother but he's not 12 yet,' said Baden.

'Hmm, difficult,' said the master, 'anyway if you want to talk, you know where I am.'

Baden wrestled with his dilemma for some days. On the one hand was his loyalty to his family and his longing to see Wales again. On the other there was his promise to Gareth Jenkins to see the world before deciding to remain in Wales for ever. And to complicate things even further there was his passionate, all-consuming love for Alejandra. Even when it came to telling Paco and Juan of his decision, the options were still revolving in his mind. Ultimately he decided to explain to them the alternatives he'd considered and hope they'd understand.

'It ought to be an easy decision. My mother needs my help and isn't it family for whom we should have our main concern and consideration?' Baden asked as he explained to the partners in their office overlooking the docks.

'Your loyalty to your family is commendable,' said Paco, 'and I don't suppose we should be surprised because it was one of the qualities we admired about you from the start.'

'So is that your decision?' asked Juan, 'you're going back to Wales?'

'I'd be lying if I didn't tell you I'm finding this very hard. Part of me feels that if I accepted your offer and stayed here Mr Jenkins would tell me I was doing just what he'd hoped I'd do; on the other hand I can also hear him saying "it's a pity you'll be so far away that you'll never see your mother or your family again."'

'And that's also true,' said Juan. Baden paused, deep in thought. Finally he drew a deep breath, and unsmiling looked each of the partners in the face before he spoke.

'There's a word in Welsh that says how I feel. It's *hiraeth*. The dictionaries describe it different ways, "nostalgia", "homesickness", "yearning" but none of them is exactly right because *hiraeth* is not exactly translatable. The best way I can describe it for you is the feeling of wanting to go home to Wales eventually. It's said to be something all Welshmen feel.'

'So, when you're old?'

'Nothing to do with age. It's to do with your heart, no matter how old it is,' said Baden.

'So you're going back to Wales?' said Juan.

Baden spread his hands in a gesture that asked the partners to understand, even if that was difficult, 'Yes. I'm sorry.'

'Why sorry? You've made your decision and we understand that,' said Paco.

'Do you? Do you really understand?' asked Baden. 'Because I know when we sail I shall watch your city and then the shores of your country disappear with my heart full of sadness. Even now as I think of myself watching the lights of Uruguay fade into the mist I shall never be sure I made the right decision.'

'We shall be sorry to see you go, Baden. Come back if ever you can, but whatever happens, never forget us,' said Paco.

'Never, you can be sure of that. Thank you, both of you.'

'Right. We part as friends and not in sorrow. Paco, may I suggest the *grappamiel*? We should drink to our promise that we never forget.'

'To the best memories,' said Paco, raising his glass.

'The best memories,' replied the other two.

The following morning the engineers announced that the ship would be ready to sail in two days' time and Baden noticed that the captain had adjusted the roster so that he would be on watch as they sailed, shortly before midnight. There was one more person he needed to see before he left and the following evening he made his way to the bar where he'd first met Alejandra. He sat at the bar and watched carefully as the patrons came and went. Eventually another attractive girl came to him and, in halting English asked if he was waiting for Alejandra. He confirmed that he was and in reply the girl wrote an address on a slip of paper and passed it to him saying 'taxi' and gestured to indicate Alejandra was crying. Baden thanked the girl and hurried outside. Fortunately a cab was waiting at the kerb. Baden handed the driver the slip of paper. He nodded and with a wave of his thumb motioned Baden to sit on the bench seat with worn out upholstery. Fifteen minutes later the cab drew up outside Alejandra's cabin. Baden paid the driver and waited, fearing he might be interrupting her with someone else. Then, in the silence of the night the door opened and his fear was unfounded for Alejandra stood before him. Her eyes were red and her eye make-up smudged so Baden knew she'd heard from Paco or Juan of his decision. Not sure what her reaction might be he remained at the side of the road until she held her hand out to him and motioned him inside.

Their lovemaking was sublime. Passionate and clinging, yet tinged with the knowledge that when the sun broke through the half-open shutters they would have to part. Their farewells were unspoken for they still shared no words for the occasion. Only when the moment came for him to dress and leave the cabin did Alejandra stand before him, their naked bodies sharing the space for one and their lips almost touching. Her eyes fastened on his as if she was memorising his face as she said the words she'd asked Paco to teach her and which she'd learnt by heart.

'When you look south at night, look up. I'll be the brightest star in the sky above you. You will always be in my heart. I will never forget you.'

The star was above him at midnight the following evening as the Alwyn Jones slipped its moorings, the capstans hauled the hawsers on board and the captain telegraphed his commands to the engine room. Slowly the vessel that had been raising steam all day got under way. Looking backwards from the wing of the bridge Baden watched until the lights of Montevideo dipped beneath the horizon and only the brightest star was left blinking its promise in the sky above. His young heart was torn, his decision made but already doubted. He knew that in his future might lie more romances, even profound relationships including one that could last a lifetime but he was also certain that he would never completely erase Alejandra from his heart and whose promise would, from time to time, flicker into his memory.

Chapter 7: Baden

In 1914 the first shots of what would later be called 'The Great War', The war to end all wars' and finally 'World War 1' were fired. At first it had little effect on people in the South Wales valleys, apart from those whose sons had already volunteered or who'd been Territorials, a scheme begun in 1908. Even when conscription was introduced by the government, most jobs in coal mining and the iron and steel industries were protected and neither Noel nor Griff was eligible to be called up. Baden, on the other hand, had signed off from the Merchant Navy after he returned from his second voyage to South America late in 1917 and was working in the family pub in Horse Street. Thus it was in June 1918 that Baden was summoned to an army camp in England and became a private in the 3rd Battalion of the Royal Fusiliers.

Although Keturah would never have shown favouritism towards any of her sons, the irony that it was her brightest boy who'd been conscripted to fight in the Army was not lost on her. Of course the fighting ceased in November 1918, when Baden was still undergoing his basic training. When he was discharged in February 1919 it was a blessing for which Keturah had silently prayed. Peace, after four years of terrible war, needed many fewer soldiers and almost all conscripts called up in 1918 were returned to civilian life. The impact on society was severe. For the thousands of men demobbed from the Army and the Navy, work was specially hard to find, but Baden was pleased because it meant he could devote all his energy to helping his mother run the Rolling Mill. What dismayed him most was the number of men, many of whom he'd grown up with in Dowlais, who allowed the enforced idleness due to a lack of jobs in the Valleys to render them unemployable. Why, he wondered, could they not see that the few men who were prepared to go where the jobs were, rather than wait for the jobs to come to them, invariably fared best.

His own respected mentor, Gareth Jenkins, had died while Baden was away on his second voyage, but he was indescribably pleased to discover that his teacher had left him inscribed copies of Mark Twain's *Huckleberry Finn*, and the 1905 translation of Gerald of Wales' *Itinerarium Cambriae, A Journey Through Wales*. Inspired not only by these gifts but also by the memory of Mr Jenkins' encouragement, Baden spent as much time as he could be spared from the pub in the Guest Memorial Library. His reading and the words of his old teacher finally led him towards an entirely different life, a life he'd never even considered before but one so different that he felt bound to explain his decision to his family one Sunday evening as they sat around the kitchen table.

'Remember why Grandpa brought you and the rest of his family to Dowlais from Carmarthen, Mam? 'Cos the work was here,' he said, answering his own question. 'And even though he'd have given anything to be back in the country, breathing clean air, he made the difficult choice because the work was here.'

'It wasn't the only reason, but yes, in the main,' added Keturah.

'And though the work was dirty and hard and dangerous, the pay was good and pretty regular.'

'At that time, but of course then there was the influx of Irish and men from Lancashire and Yorkshire...,' interjected Noel.

'All of which drove down our wages,' added Griff.

'Right, but the unions eventually got organised and forced the owners to pay decent rates,' said Noel, warming to his subject as an active union man.

'But then it all began to go downhill, Mam,' declared Baden.

'You've obviously been giving this a lot of thought son', said his mother.

'I have Mam, because it seems to me that whatever we've got in Wales won't last for ever.'

'That's nonsense boy,' said Noel loudly. 'Wales, South Wales at least, is made of coal. There's millions of tons of it left under our feet. It'll last for centuries. You're daft Baden, South America's gone to your head, boy.'

'Hear me out, Noel. Yes, you may be right, maybe Wales is made of coal that we can dig out for centuries to come, but at what price and what's the quality? Don't tell me it's all anthracite 'cos we know it's not, and the next question is what will it cost to get out? That's why the English are coming here from Lancashire, the seams there are so narrow that there's so much dirt, it's almost not worth digging it out. And they're already talking about Wales running out of iron ore and importing it from Spain.'

'So what?'

'So what will we do if they decide to leave the iron ore in Spain and ship our coal out there? That'll mean more jobs in Spain and fewer jobs here.'

'Seems like you know it all, Baden,' said Griff. 'Maybe you should go to London and tell the government.'

'Not me *bach* but who's to say they'll not find coal in Poland or India or China, and last of all, are you sure they'll not invent machines that run on something other than coal?' asked Baden.

'On what? There's nothing I ever heard of that's better than steam and that takes coal,' answered Noel.

'I don't know, Noel, but I'm not prepared to swear that someday something else won't come along other than coal and steam, and then what will we do? What will we do if no one wants coal anymore? If that happens there'll be grass growing in the streets of Dowlais, mark my words. Green grass.'

Looking back years later, Keturah remembered she'd been born into a world of farming where change was gradual, driven by the land, the crops and animals, and the seasons. Now change was like the River Taff in springtime when the winter snow on the Beacons melted and water swelled the river and burst down the valley. Everything in her life that had seemed certain just a few years ago was now uncertain and she wondered if she was ready for the changes the years would bring.

Later that evening it was very quiet in the pub and Baden was alone with his mother, clearly worried that her son, so recently returned to her, would be leaving again. Speaking quietly, she returned to the subject the family had discussed earlier.

'What's made you think like this Baden *bach*?'

'It was something Mr Jenkins said before I took the exam for Cyfarthfa.'

'Go on.'

'He said two things, actually. First, that all learning has some value, some purpose and use. Second, that the younger you are when you learn the more valuable it is.'

'So what you going to do?'

'Get the best education I can.'

'Where d'you do that and who pays for it?'

'Ironically, in the Army.'

'The Army?' exclaimed Keturah, 'I thought all they teach you is to march, to shoot and kill.'

'Marching for sure, but I think that after four years of war and millions dead even the Army's fed up with shooting and killing. Their education is as good an education as I'll get anywhere and it's free,' declared Baden proudly.

'Free? How come son?'

'Well, I'll have to sign on for six years. During that time they feed me, house me, clothe me and educate me.'

'And in those six years they can send you to fight anywhere they want?' added his mother.

'It's possible but my sense is that the world's had enough of killing for now. Of course, there are no guarantees in life but I think I'll be joining a peacetime army, an army that needs educated soldiers not men to die in trenches.'

'And after six years? What then?' asked Keturah, nervously wringing her hands.

'I think, as Mr Jenkins said, the world will still be my oyster. I'll still only be 26 and the world will still be there for me to discover.'

To Keturah, her son sounded like eternal youth–optimistic, positive and if not entirely carefree, certain he could take on whatever the world threw at him.

A few days later he went to Cardiff and presented himself to a recruiting sergeant who persuaded him to opt for the Welsh Guards rather than an ordinary infantry regiment.

'Big lad from the Valleys like you ought to join the Welsh Guards, boy. Tall bearskin, lovely red tunic, all the pretty girls go for a guardsman. Leave the others for the guys in khaki,' he said, and so Baden signed up to join the 1ˢᵗ Battalion, Welsh Guards. Fortunately it was a decision that he never regretted, even when he discovered that the recruiting sergeant earned sixpence for recruiting a private soldier but ninepence for signing up a guardsman.

Chapter 8: Keturah and Gloria

One might have expected that since the family had already twice bade their son and brother farewell, sending him off to Aldershot would be easy, but it wasn't. Noel and Griff said their goodbyes as they left for work early in the morning but Keturah, Millie, Lila and Daniel all went down to Dowlais station to see Baden off. As he looked at his younger siblings, now grown up into young adults, standing on the platform, Baden thought to himself how it felt as though he'd somehow missed their childhoods while he was away. Millie was already the quieter, more introspective of his sisters. Lila, her younger sister, was more vivacious, even feisty. She certainly had a string of young admirers competing for her smile. Despite the slight facial disfigurement left over from his childhood acne, Danny–the youngest– child had grown into a slim, engaging young man, constantly in the shadow of his older sisters but committed to helping his mother as she grew older.

As the train puffed into the station the family's last hugs and kisses were hurried and nervous, and Baden was aware of his mother's firm grip on his arm.

'Take care my son. Don't forget us,' she sobbed, as Millie wrapped her arm around her mother's shoulder, nodding a silent assurance to Baden that she'd make sure their mother was OK.

After his initial training Baden joined his battalion at Chelsea Barracks where it would be based for most of his service. Raised in 1915 on the Western Front, once the war was over the Welsh Guards were most visible in their ceremonial duties in London. Preparing for these ceremonial duties meant even more soldiering before Baden could start to get the education he'd hoped for and had been promised when he signed on for six years' service.

As Keturah had recognised, but Baden had dismissed when he told his family he was joining the army, much can happen in six years.

Although Baden's principal objective in doing so had been to get an education, there were also the usual (and more strenuous), aspects of army life as well. He boxed for his squad, earning two knockouts before getting a broken nose that ended his boxing career. It also made him snore for the rest of his life. The social life of the Guards was also very active and even junior non-commissioned officers were occasionally expected to engage in some of the events. With all the necessities of life provided by the Army, and ceremonial duties regulating his life he was able to indulge himself as a single man with the two great temptations facing men in his situation, drinking and gambling. While he remained subject to the discipline of the Army his drinking, at least, was to some extent controlled, but gambling became a costly habit that would stay with him all his life.

In early 1924 Baden also met the woman who would become his wife. Nellie Trebilcock, who preferred to be called Gloria, or Glory, was the daughter of a licensee whose pub lay on the borders of Chelsea and Fulham. Gloria was 32, some eight years older than Baden, and consequently she was more experienced than he was. Their courtship was frenetic, even by military standards. Gloria's experience of life in an urban environment in the capital left Baden's almost rural maturity far behind. From her point of view Baden was a handsome, socially-acceptable young man, still relatively untouched by life in the capital. Gloria decided that although she'd allowed her previous love affairs to dwindle to nothing that would not happen in this case. Using all her feminine wiles and intuition, she drove their romance forward. On 27th December 1924 and with little advance notice, she and Baden were married at the church of St Dionis in Parsons Green. It all happened so quickly there was no time for anyone in Dowlais to attend, and the family only found out when Baden wrote a long letter home. Indeed, it crossed Keturah's mind that perhaps Baden and Gloria had had to get married. She mentioned her concern to Millie.

'What? You mean she was pregnant, Mam?' exclaimed Millie. 'No. I don't believe it.'

'It happens my love. Think about your great grandmother Caroline.'

'But not Baden, surely....'

'He's a lovely man and a dear brother, I know, but that doesn't make him a saint.'

Millie smiled, slightly embarrassed by her mother's frankness. Her mother continued, 'I know he's not said a lot about his girlfriend in Montevideo, what was her name now?'

'Alejandra, Mam, like Alexandra,' prompted Millie.

'That's right, but I don't think she was a Mother Superior.'

'I know what you mean, Mam, but he was really in love with her I think.'

'Well, we'll never know now, that's for sure,' said Keturah folding the letter from Baden.

Had she known the full story, Keturah would have been even more upset about Baden's marriage, for Gloria's family environment drew Baden back towards the life he'd avoided so far, the life in which drink and drunkenness, cigarettes, cigars and smoking were normal. With permission from his senior officer Baden was able to take private lodgings away from the barracks with his new wife and they subsequently lived at a number of rented properties in Windsor, and in the Parsons Green and Fulham areas of West London.

As Keturah had feared when her son left for London, although the threat of conventional conflict receded after the Great War, civil unrest occasionally erupted and dealing with it involved the army. During the General Strike of 1926, shortly before the end of his tour of service, Baden (by now a corporal) was detailed to guard a lorry delivering copies of *The British Gazette* to various distribution points around London. The printers were one of the first industries to be called out on strike by the TUC. Since newspapers were still the principal means of disseminating information to the public, the government decided to print its own newspaper carrying official news of the strike. Winston Churchill, then Chancellor of the

Exchequer but formerly a journalist, was appointed editor. Baden's orders that day were to protect the lorry and its consignment of newspapers, but without exacerbating the public mood. Accordingly he ordered his soldiers to use only the butts of their rifles and then only if the lorry was attacked by strikers.

While Baden was making his way in the Welsh Guards others in the Howells family were getting on with their lives too. Shortly after Baden had enlisted in the army Noel had met an English girl from the Shropshire borders and fallen in love. Marie Louise Cope was utterly besotted with Noel but upset at the prospect of living anywhere in the Welsh Valleys. Consequently her family, well-connected in the Welsh Borders, found Noel a job on a farm near Shrewsbury, and they were married in 1922.

Two years later, depressed by the worsening conditions in the Valleys, Griff asked his mother how she would feel if he emigrated to America.

'America? The United States? *Duw*, I never did,' she exclaimed. 'Where did you get that idea boy?'

'Robert, Dewi Evans, the carpenter's son. Went over two years ago. Got set up with a good carpentry job in Ohio. Now he's sending back so much money his Dada's talking about retiring.'

'And are there any good jobs in iron and steel works in America?'

'I don't know Mam but if I have to learn a new trade then I'll learn,' said Griff confidently.

'It's like everything our Baden was saying about Wales changing is coming true,' she said quietly. 'Whatever next?'

'Well, I'll need some help, Mam.'

'What sort of help son?'

'With the fare.'

'And how can I help, Griff? I'm still paying back the bank after your Dada cleared out almost all my savings the last time he came home.'

'I know about that. I've got some savings that I think make up what Dada took.'

'And then what?'

'I thought maybe you could get a loan on the pub, the

business not the house, and I'll send you back money every month to repay it.'

'But supposing you can't get work?'

'I'm sure I will, absolutely certain, and if necessary I'll borrow it over there to pay you back. I won't let you down, promise.'

'Well, I don't know Griff....'

'I'll do it official like, in writing. Tell you what, ask the others, the girls and Danny, Baden and Noel too if you want. If they don't agree I won't go.'

As it turned out all the children, except Noel who didn't reply to his mother's letter at all, agreed to lend Griff money for the fare provided he signed a legal contract to repay his mother. Thus, in early summer of 1924, Griff sailed from Liverpool to New York where he took a train to Cleveland and met up with Robert Evans. He found a job almost immediately and at the end of his second month in the US started sending his mother money orders as he'd promised. He got married too. At a Welsh community club he met an Irish girl whose mother was originally from North Wales. The attraction was immediate, mutual, and passionate. Within six months they were married. Back in Dowlais his family were delighted, not so much with his choice of bride, for Kathleen was a Catholic, but because they felt that being married would give him some stability.

Millie had found work as a seamstress at the house of one of the principal investors in the company that had recently bought out both the original Cyfarthfa Ironworks and the Dowlais Iron and Steelworks. A serious but reliable girl she eventually married Morgan James from a Dowlais colliery family. They had one son, Griff, born just before the second world war.

Lila, Millie's sister was as different from her as chalk from cheese. Lively, uninhibited, opinionated and sometimes rebellious to the point of seeming Bohemian, she had a succession of boyfriends in her youth. Sadly, perhaps taking more after her father than her

107

mother, she took a variety of unskilled jobs wherever she could find them and eventually had three husbands but no children with any of them.

Initially it seemed that during the early 1920s the family managed to rub along pretty well together, even though they didn't see a great deal of each other. It wasn't to last. Not only did Keturah hear nothing of Davy from one year to the next, but as the 1920s wore on more family catastrophes were waiting in line and Keturah had to face them alone.

In 1925, Danny, Keturah's youngest child, contracted scarlet fever. No-one knew how, since he was the only child in the whole of Dowlais in whom the disease was diagnosed. He suffered in the isolation ward of Merthyr Hospital but died on 6th September. Sadly neither her husband nor her other sons could get to Dowlais for Danny's funeral and burial on the hillside at Pant though Baden sent a postal order that covered most of the cost of the headstone that Keturah had erected on Danny's grave.

It was two years before Davy appeared in Dowlais again. Danny's death was a complete surprise and a hammer-blow to his father. Worse, Davy objected to the fact that Keturah had omitted his name from Danny's headstone.

     '"Beloved son of Keturah Howells" it says. Didn't he have a bloody father?'

     'Of course he had a father Davy,' said Keturah incensed at her husband's gall and insensitivity. 'It's just that his father hadn't been here for years when his son died–so long I don't think the lad remembered what his father even looked like.'

     'I want my name on that stone. He's my son as much as yours.'

     'Then pay for it. Have it put on like a postscript, an afterthought. Run it round the edge. No-one will expect it to be visible any more than you were visible when he was alive.'

'No. You can damned well pay for a new one, with my name written proper.'

'Can't happen, Davy.'

'What's stopping you?'

'I didn't pay for it. I couldn't afford for a headstone for my own son,' she started to sob.

'Then who did, Father Christmas?'

'No!' she shrieked so unexpectedly and out of character, 'Baden sent me the money!'

'Then I don't suppose he'll mind paying for his father's name to be added.'

'I wouldn't count on it Davy Howells–I wouldn't count on it,' she said angrily.

In fact, when Baden heard of his father's outburst at his mother he sent money to the stone mason and had him add, in the same typeface but out of alignment, 'D and' in front of Keturah's name, there not being enough space to include 'David and'. Thus his father's wish was met but no-one who knew the family was under any illusion why the inscription looked so odd.

The family did hear from Noel the following year when his first son, Valentine Noel Howells was born, on 23rd June 1926 at Margam near Port Talbot. Millie replied on Keturah's behalf (since their mother's written English wasn't good), congratulating Noel and Marie on the birth of their son. She explained how surprised they were that Noel and his wife were back in South Wales and brought them up to date with the remainder of the family news. Noel didn't reply but just before Christmas that year Marie wrote a brief, rather abject letter to Keturah from Shropshire, to where she'd returned. She explained that shortly after their son's birth Noel had packed his bag and walked from their house announcing his intention to emigrate to New Zealand, leaving his wife and son behind. Since then she'd not heard anything of her husband at all but with help from her family was managing to raise their son herself.

Exactly 20 days before Valentine was born, his Uncle Griffith died 4,000 miles away in Cleveland, Ohio. Griff, of course, had not been a strong child and had suffered with generally poor health for much of his adult life. That was perhaps why he succumbed to tuberculosis, a common disease responsible for about half of all adults under 55 years old in the United States at that time. Griff's death had a profound effect on the family, for at a stroke repayment of the mortgage Keturah had raised on her business to fund his journey to the USA ceased. Fortunately the lender had no lien on her home, just the licensed business that the new owner moved to another premises elsewhere in Dowlais. Nevertheless it was a severe blow to Keturah. Two of her sons had died, a third had abandoned his wife, child and country, and she hadn't heard from her own husband in 10 years. Her two daughters still lived nearby but had their own homes and husbands to care for. Keturah viewed the future without much optimism.

Her concerns were soon eased. Shortly after she'd begun to come to terms with the tragic news from America, Keturah received a very welcome letter from the company holding a mortgage on her home. Fortunately, when Davy's parents died, leaving him the ownership of their pub, he'd quite uncharacteristically used the proceeds to pay off almost all the outstanding debt on 1 Horse Street. Of course, this didn't affect the loss of their business that had resulted from Griff's untimely death, but did mean that Keturah still had a roof over her head.

With Britain–like the rest of the world–in the grip of recession, Baden decided his most prudent course of action was to sign on for a second 6-year tour of duty with the Welsh Guards. However, almost as soon as he had done so it was announced that the 1st Battalion would be going to Egypt. Although it would prove to be only a temporary move, to avoid this disruption to his home life Baden transferred to the reserve, which remained in London. Before the completion of his first tour Baden had already been awarded his

1ˢᵗ class Certificate of Education. As he wrote to his mother, the success more than justified his decision to get his education in the Army. Even more significantly, later that year after he'd been promoted to Sergeant, he was awarded a 'Distinguished' pass on the 16ᵗʰ course of education at Shorncliffe Barracks, enabling him to become an army teacher.

Although Baden was nominally still based in London, the various different bases around the UK to which he was posted disrupted his home life and led to arguments and disagreements with Gloria. She began to drink heavily and, with many of her old friends still socialising at her parents' pub, eventually she started seeing other people. Even when Baden was at home, Gloria's reluctance to have a family (on the grounds that she'd have little help in bringing up children) added to the strain in their marriage.

In 1932, as the end of Baden's second tour approached, he discussed with his wife whether he should stay in the Army or leave and start a new career as a civilian. His problem was that apart from his qualification as a teacher, he had few skills that could be transferred directly to civilian life. In some desperation, for she feared Baden would sign on for a third tour, Gloria suggested that they should look for a pub to manage together. That wasn't a good idea, as they both knew from family experience, but before making a decision he turned to an older publican he respected and had become very close to at Gloria's father's pub, Arthur Nice.

Arthur Nice was licensee of the White Hart public house at Chalvey, then a village outside Slough in Berkshire, west of London. The building was already old–the date-stone recorded it being built in 1861. With his plump, cheery wife, Gladys, Arthur ran a prosperous and popular business despite the age of the building. Arthur and Baden had got on well from the outset and having known Gloria since she was a young girl Arthur was able to sympathise with Baden when his wife's demands became unreasonable and excessive.

111

When Baden had persuaded his wife that going back into the licensed trade wouldn't do either of them, or their relationship, any good, Gloria related the experience of another of the friends she'd made before they were married.

'Charlie's working for a top solicitor in the city now. He's not got formal qualifications, just a lot of common sense and the gift of the gab,' she told Baden.

'Where do you see jobs like that advertised is what I'd like to know,' said Baden.

'I've no idea,' said Gloria, 'why don't you ask Charlie?'

When they met, Baden discovered that Charlie was really little more than an office boy running errands and that he relied on his gift of the gab more than any other skills. Nevertheless, what Baden did notice in the various solicitors' offices Charlie took him to as he delivered his employer's messages was that each of them had a number of clerks working through various piles of paper and documents. At one office Charlie had to leave him and Baden, having first apologised for interrupting one of the clerks, took the opportunity to ask exactly what he was doing.

'Me? I'm just putting all the letters, memos and chargeable documents for this case into date order before they're sent over to the law costs draftsman,' he replied.

'Over to who?' asked Baden.

'The law costs draftsman,' said the clerk.

'What exactly does he do?'

'Well, he goes through the file page by page, item by item, making a note of everything we can charge to the other side–because in this case we won the case for our client–and then adding it up.'

'Does he decide how much each item costs?'

'No,' the clerk laughed, 'there's a fixed cost for each type of item, so much for a letter, so much for a telephone call, and so on.'

'And that's it?' said Baden.

'Pretty much. He has to take the bill before the Taxing

Master who checks that it's accurate and that he agrees the biggest variable charge in any bill, which is for briefing the counsel, is a fair amount. Of course the other side's law costs draftsman will be arguing that it's too much but then that's the game, isn't it?'

'Fascinating,' said Baden with the germ of an idea already forming in his mind.

Back at home Baden told Gloria about his visit to Charlie and the conversation with the solicitor's clerk. 'I think I could do that,' he said.

'Give it a try', said Gloria. 'You know what they say, nothing ventured nothing gained.'

And so it was that Baden, son of a stonemason-turned-publican, a ship's cook and merchant seaman, teacher and soldier made another change in the direction of his life, this time a change that would last him the rest of his life.

Although Gloria had supported his decision to start a new career, the hours he spent knocking on doors of solicitors' offices around the city eventually impinged too much on the time he was at home and led to more arguments, more disagreements and more unpleasantness. It all came to a head one day in June 1934 when Gloria demanded that Baden took her away on holiday the following week.

'I haven't had a proper holiday since Easter last year. You're never at home, you're either out visiting contacts or you've got your head stuck in piles of paper.'

'Look Gloria, I've got to get this job done in time. You knew it would be a struggle to get my business started, I just need a bit more time and a bit more support.'

'Well, I'm fed up with supporting you,' she said. 'If you don't want to go on holiday with me, I'll find someone who does.'

Nothing more was said but two weeks later Baden came home to find a handwritten note from Gloria telling him that she'd be away for a couple of weeks 'having a holiday and some fun'. Thinking she'd gone with one of her girlfriends he was disappointed but not excessively worried. That all changed when Gloria came home.

'Hello darling. Have a good time?' he enquired as she opened the door.

'Fabulous, just fabulous. That Charlie really knows how to give a girl a good time.'

There was a pause as Baden absorbed the implication of what his wife had just said. 'Charlie? I assumed you were going with one of your girlfriends.'

'I could have done but Charlie was around and had the time off himself so we went together.'

'I don't want to sound like a lovesick teenager but I feel bound to ask, did you stay together?' asked Baden.

'Of course we did. Nobody knows either of us in Bournemouth and having separate rooms would just be an unnecessary expense. I did tell you what I was going to do. You had your chance.'

'You didn't say you'd be going with Charlie, or any other man for that matter.'

'Well, that's your fault for making the wrong assumptions,' she said with a shrug of her shoulders.

'So what happens now?' asked Baden.

'Well, I'm home refreshed by a good holiday.'

'And Charlie?'

'Who knows?' she said. 'We had a good time but I'm not interested in him long term and I think he feels the same about me.'

Two days later after a couple of telephone calls to Arthur Nice, Baden packed his bags, took a train to Slough and a taxi to the White Hart, where he wrote a letter to his mother giving her his new address.

Chapter 10: David and Connie

Despite separating from his wife, life that summer was good for Baden. He had a small room up a few stairs from Arthur and Gladys' family quarters above the pub. He had plenty to keep him busy, drawing up lists of potential clients from the legal directories, telephoning for appointments and going up to town to keep the meetings he'd arranged. The only disadvantage to living in a pub, given his family background, was the temptation to start drinking again.

The summer proved to be exquisite in other ways as well, one of those balmy summers we always remember even when we forget about the rainy, cold and wet ones. And it wasn't just the weather he enjoyed. One day Arthur Nice's wife, Gladys, remarked to Baden, 'you'll have to be on your best behaviour next week my lad.'

'I'm always on my best behaviour Gladys, but what's so special next week?'

'We've got someone else coming to stay for a week or so. Daughter of an old friend of mine from Paddington.'

'Want me to move out?'

'No, you're OK. I've known her mother for years, almost since we were girls ourselves. She can have our daughter's room after I've cleared out the boxes. She'll not disturb you.'

That proved to be the contradiction of the century for the girl who arrived the following week didn't disturb Baden, just turned his whole world upside down. But it wasn't easy.

The afternoon that Connie arrived Baden was working his way through a long bill trying to spot why the Taxing Master had rejected it for inaccuracy. He heard a light footstep on the stairs and then became aware of someone watching him.

'Sorry. I didn't mean to disturb you,' said a girl wearing a fashionable blouse and skirt and with gently bobbed and waved hair.

'I was looking for Auntie Gladys.'

'You weren't disturbing me, so no apology necessary. And I'm sorry,' he said looking around and under the table, 'Gladys isn't up here either.'

'Thanks,' she smiled politely but unamused, 'I'll let you get on,' and she turned away and disappeared into another part of the family quarters.

Arthur and Gladys had long been accustomed to having their dinner early in the evening, before the pub opened. Baden had dropped into the same routine whenever he was at the pub. On days when he was in London he bought himself a meal in the City before coming home. So, that evening he was already seated when Connie walked into the family kitchen.

'Hello again,' he said.

'Hello.'

'I assume you found your aunt this afternoon?' He asked politely.

'Yes thank you. She was in the potting shed with Uncle Arthur.'

'Very Lady Chatterley,' he said and immediately regretted the suggestive joke. 'Sorry, bad joke. Excuse me.'

'To be honest I didn't understand it anyway.'

'No harm done then. Aunt Gladys mentioned that you live in Paddington,' he said, changing the subject.

'Yes.'

'Like it there?'

'That part of London's all I've ever known.'

'Do you like this weather or is it too hot for you?'

'It suits me.'

'Do you work?'

'Yes, of course.'

'Interesting job?'

'It can be, sometimes.'

'I work too.'

'Really, that's interesting.'

'Is it?'

'I expect so.'

'I'm not sure how long Arthur and Gladys are going to be so I think I'll go to my room until they come up from the bar,' said Baden, tired of a conversation that Connie seemed determined to ensure was going nowhere.

'I'll tell them if they ask,' she said.

'If it's no trouble,' he replied.

'None at all.'

'Thanks.'

'Right.'

Back in his room Baden wondered where on earth Arthur and Gladys had discovered this girl. No conversation, almost monosyllabic responses to any question he asked. Could she have any compensating qualities, he wondered.

In the event Arthur and Gladys were so late coming upstairs that they only had time for a quick sandwich. Two police constables had arrived to discuss a minor fracas that had happened earlier at another pub half a mile down the road. A report had been made that suggested the lads (and that's all they were) had headed towards the White Hart later. They hadn't, but these young policemen evidently had to ask all their questions at least twice.

'I'm sorry you and Baden were delayed. You should have started without us,' said Gladys.

'I think Baden went out to get something. I haven't seen him since he made his apologies and left the table,' said Connie.

'Did you like him?' asked Gladys.

'We didn't really talk much. He asked a lot of questions but didn't tell me much.'

'Maybe he was shy.'

'That wasn't how he struck me, Auntie. Rather full of himself if you ask me, and very nosey.'

'Maybe he had something on his mind. He's recently

separated. Left his wife after she had an affair with another man.'

'Perhaps she found his conversation too exciting to remain.'

Connie wasn't a naturally evasive person, indeed most friends, male and female, found her stimulating company, easy to engage and an attentive listener. She'd recently ended an engagement to be married to Jimmy, an engineer in the telephone exchange at which she worked. He was attentive, convivial and good company but she'd not become engaged because she was in love, rather because it seemed the conventional next step to do. Having ended that relationship, Connie wasn't about to get involved with a married man, even one who was separated from his wife. Right then, that was the last temptation she wanted to face.

Not that this Baden wasn't good-looking, he was, she couldn't deny that–and very much better looking than past-tense Jimmy. But getting over Jimmy was top of her list of things to do this week and she decided that, if properly handled, good-looking Baden might be a useful antidote. If he didn't ride a motorbike either–one of Jimmy's passions–he'd already risen another step up her 'ladder of approval'.

Good-looking Baden didn't appear all day, or rather–according to Uncle Arthur–he'd left on the early train to keep his first appointment in the City. Surely, she thought, he doesn't describe himself as 'Something in the City'. Well, she'd see about that. Instead she wrote a postcard to her mother who was taking a holiday without her father in St Leonards. She didn't mention the young Welshman, though she did make a mental note about St Leonards as 'another destination to cross off my list'. Instead she bought a cartoon postcard, intending to send it later that evening to her very much younger sister–a child who, Connie was certain, was her parents' accidental last fling.

The following day dawned bright, clear and optimistic, as long as you ignored the old saw about red skies in the morning warning shepherds. Connie bathed and dressed in a white pleated dress, white tennis shoes and tied a royal blue scarf loosely around her throat, a shade that she knew accentuated the colour of her eyes. Baden was already at the kitchen table drinking a strong coffee and smoking a cigarette. His striped blazer and fawn slacks with matching slip-on shoes were the clearest indication that he wasn't going 'up to town' that day.

'Good morning,' he said, half rising in his chair.

'Good morning,' replied Connie, 'don't get up.'

'I hoped we might get off on a better footing today,' said Baden folding his newspaper and laying it to one side. 'I must have seemed a bit clumsy the other day.'

'It was probably as much my fault,' smiled Connie, 'I'm not very good at small talk with people I've only just met.'

'Well that's good then. We met the other day so we can carry on from there. My name's Baden.'

'I'm Connie. Well, Constance really but my mother only calls me that when I'm in trouble. Nice to meet you Baden.'

'Likewise.'

'Could you pass the milk jug, please? I don't think I've met a Baden before. It's unusual, even for London.'

'It's fairly unusual even for Wales.'

'Is that where you're from?'

'Yes, Dowlais actually.'

'I thought you had an accent but I've not heard of Dowlais I'm afraid. Perhaps it's a small village,' said Connie buttering a slice of toast.

'Iron and steel capital of the world, according to the papers.'

'Sorry. I'm not very well up on iron and steel towns.'

'So where's your accent from then?'

'I don't really have an accent now, that's been trained out of me, but as you know I was brought up in Paddington in West London.'

'I've no idea what a Paddington accent sounds like but how do you get your voice trained and anyway, why?'

119

'I'm a GPO telephonist and part of our training is to make us sound as clear as possible.'

'Fascinating. Give me an example, if you don't mind.'

'I don't mind but it'll sound very odd to you just sitting here. It only sounds right over a telephone line.'

'So what you're saying is that I should go into Slough and telephone you from there?' he smiled, and she responded with a laugh. 'It's good to see you laugh,' he said. 'Have you something planned for the rest of the morning?' Baden asked as Connie dabbed away the crumbs from her lips with her napkin.

'Nothing definite. I was planning to visit Eton and maybe Windsor.'

'Then would you allow me to accompany you to Eton? We'll take the bus and, if you'd like, I'll row you on the river.'

'Are you qualified to do that?' she asked, cautiously and quite seriously.

'It's funny you should ask,' he smiled wryly, 'I'm completely untrained on buses but I'm actually half-qualified and quite safe on the river–plus I know seventeen nautical words in Spanish if it helps you decide.'

By the end of the week David (she'd already told him she felt sure she'd never come to terms with calling anyone Baden) and Connie knew pretty much all there was to know about each other on a superficial level. They'd covered the easy bits; their likes and dislikes, hobbies and families, animals and–in Connie's case–her irrational fear of spiders. They'd also ventured on to tougher subjects, in unspecific terms at least; love, marriage, truth, honesty, fairness and responsibility. At the end of the week they parted, both anxious and hoping that they'd left the right impression and each as determined as the other that, if things continued as they'd begun, their stars might burn together for a long time.

Author's notes

This short volume was originally conceived not as a novel at all but as an early chapter in my memoir. Unfortunately because my father's divorce from his first wife was so fraught, he and his second wife, my mother, spoke very little about his early life. Indeed, even the fact that he had been married before was only revealed to me on my 21st birthday. I was curious about my father's early history but it was clear that neither of my parents wanted to say much if anything about it.

Years later, Niki, my wife, made some valuable discoveries among the various archives and official records but the information was sparse and basic and, as I learned later, prone to inaccuracy. Rather than include in my memoir what would be little more than the notes that already exist in our Family Tree, I decided to indulge my interest and modest skill in storytelling and invent what wasn't in the official records–in other words, to write a novel.

It also enabled me to delve into the effect we, as individuals, have on our own lives and the lives of those we touch along the way, a theme I first explored in my novel *Passing Unseen*. In that respect, although this volume deals with part of the story I've told in my memoir, it is a departure from the memoir which, as far as possible, deals with facts and not supposition. Serendipity might account for the situations we reach in our journey through life but it is often simple, unforeseen decisions that set or re-direct the path we follow. The decision Baden made not to become a ship's chandler in Montevideo (Alejandra was an invention of mine), the decision Connie made to spend an unexpected week's holiday at The White Hart and thus meet Baden, are examples of what I mean.

Because it is a mixture of fact and fiction, to help members of my family for whom I've written my memoir, I should identify the

122

elements of this novel that are true; and those that are wholly or partially invented. Of course, all the dialogue is imagined, that goes without saying.

Of my ancestors I have documented proof of the existence of the following people:

Caroline Lewis: my great-great-grandmother,

Amelia Lewis: Caroline's daughter and my great-grandmother,

Griffith Thomas: Amelia's husband,

Keturah Thomas: Amelia and Griffith's older daughter and my paternal grandmother,

Rebecca, David and James Thomas: Amelia and Griffith's other children,

David William Howells (called Davy in the novel to avoid confusion): my paternal grandfather,

David Baden Howells: Keturah and Davy's third child and my father,

William Noel, Griffith Thomas, Elizabeth (Lila), Daniel, and Amelia (Millie) Howells: Keturah and Davy's other children and their spouses,

Valentine Noel Howells: William Noel and Marie Louise Cope's son and my cousin,

Griff: Amelia's son and my cousin.

Where specific dates or places have been mentioned they are as accurate as the documents from which they were obtained. This caveat applies especially to Welsh census returns which, in the late 19th and early 20th centuries especially, were invariably completed by Englishmen who didn't speak Welsh. Further, due to the social stigma regarding the language(s) people spoke, census returns were documents on which people sometimes gave inaccurate information.

I've researched the geography and established the probable site of Troedyrhiw Farm in Abernant and visited Ffoeshelig Farm (which still stands) in Newchurch. Abernant School from the period also stands but is now a private domestic property. Goose Street in

Carmarthen still exists but has been re-named, St Catherine Street. Dowlais has been re-developed twice since my family lived there. Old maps held by Dowlais Library show the original sites. Horse Street no longer exists, nor of course does The Rolling Mill at No. 1 in that street. Mount Pleasant Street still exists though the Moriah Chapel that once stood there has been demolished. All the other streets and addresses in Glamorgan that are mentioned are extant. So too is Cyfarthfa Castle in Merthyr Tydfil. When I visited it during the 1980s the school shared the building with a museum that now occupies the entire building.

My father told me with some certainty that he made two voyages to South America and was offered a partnership in a ship's chandler's in Montevideo and although, as I've noted, Alejandra is one of my invented characters, I don't think finding someone like her in my father's story is beyond the bounds of possibility. I have no idea how seriously Baden considered remaining in Montevideo, though had he done so his story would have had a very different ending and I might never have written this.

Finally, I should record that David and Connie did fall in love, lived together and, in 1941, got married. They had two sons. In late 1943 they moved from the London suburbs to West Sussex where they lived for the rest of their lives. By the time he died of cancer, aged 67, in November 1967, David had become one of the most respected law costs draftsmen in the High Court. Connie eventually forsook her London origins and in later life described herself as 'a Sussex woman'. She died in October 2005 aged 94.

Translation of Welsh words and phrases used in the volume

Ach-y-fi	Nonsense, rubbish, yuck
Bach	Small, dear, diminutive or familiar suffix
Baban	Baby
Cariad	Love, lover, sweetheart
Cymanfa Ganu	Welsh choral singing festival
Dada	Dad
Dai	Diminutive or familiar of David
Diolch	Thanks
Diolch yn fawr	Thanks very much
Duw	God
Fy caru	My love
Mam	Mum
Nain	Grandma
Nos da	Goodnight

Translation of Spanish words and phrases used in the volume

Comiendo	Eating
Entiendo	I understand
La cocina del barco	The ship's kitchen or galley
Madre de Dios	Mother of God (Common blasphemy)
No bebé.	No baby
No voy a quedar embarazada	I won't get pregnant
No habla...	I don't speak...
Por favor	Please
¿Qué es tan difícil?	What's so difficult?
¿Qué?	What?
Señor	Sir (as form of address)
Sí	Yes
Soy el velero	I am the chandler

Books by Philip Howells, all available from Amazon.

A Small Injury

A Distinctive Flourish

Passing Unseen

Short Stories Vol 1

'I'll Be The Brightest Star...'

Rufus T Weeks (coming soon)

Printed in Poland
by Amazon Fulfillment
Poland Sp. z o.o., Wrocław